Kate Field

Ten days in Spain

Kate Field

Ten days in Spain

ISBN/EAN: 9783337229207

Printed in Europe, USA, Canada, Australia, Japan

Cover: Foto ©Andreas Hilbeck / pixelio.de

More available books at **www.hansebooks.com**

Ten Days in Spain.

BY

KATE FIELD.

Illustrated.

BOSTON:
JAMES R. OSGOOD AND COMPANY,
Late Ticknor & Fields, and Fields, Osgood, & Co.
1875.

Dedicated,

IN SWEET REVENGE,

TO

THE BLINKER.

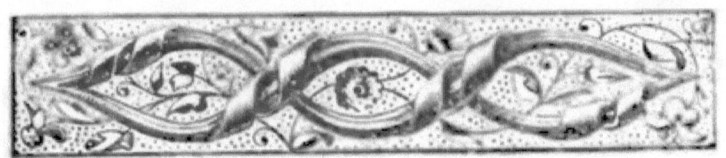

Contents.

PART V.

EMILIO CASTELAR.

PART VI.

THE ESCORIAL AND TOLEDO.

PART VII.

LAST DAY IN MADRID.

PART VIII.

CROSSING THE FRONTIER.

PART IX.

LAST DAY OF ALL.

Illustrations.

PART I.

By Way of Introduction.

I.

Rain in the Pyrenees. — Concerning Biarritz. — Plan of entering Spain. — A Prudent Journalist. — Untrustworthy Couriers. — Conciliating Public Opinion.

FOR six weeks I had been walking about on the top of the Pyrenees, with a glass of lukewarm water in one hand and an umbrella in the other, with long parentheses of going to bed, and short parentheses of sitting down and putting my feet in a foot-muff. It is one of many fictions that the summer heat of the Pyrenees is excessive, and that rain is unknown. I experienced no heat, and underwent much rain. It was an exceptional season. I never went anywhere that the season was not exceptional,

and am convinced that in all climates excep-
tions do not prove, but are, the rule. Lukewarm water, combined with umbrella and foot-
muffs, does not inebriate, neither does it cheer.
In fact, another week of it would have driven
me to the verge of a neighborly precipice, perpetually inviting me to a hollow embrace. The
Heights of the Pyrenees were the depths of my
despair, and Monsieur le Médécin at last told
me I had accomplished my cure and might go.
Blessed release !

But what should I do to restore my brain to
its normal condition? I had been at the top
of things; I would go to the bottom. "Come
to Biarritz," urged French friends. Biarritz was
as near bottom as I could go without drowning
myself in the Atlantic Ocean. As I had just
kept my head above water all summer, I thought
I had nearly been drowned enough. I would
go to Biarritz and have it off my mind. What-

ever place you have never seen is precisely the place set down as the earthly paradise by those Superior Beings who have been everywhere. You cannot contradict them, though certain that they are as untrustworthy as historians. They know their advantage, and sit upon you with an amount of ecstatic information that makes you loathe Average Intelligence, and wish the common variety of traveller as extinct as a retired American President. I had suffered from Biarritz for several years. It was time for the patient worm to turn and rend the travelled bore. "And when I have digested Biarritz," said I to myself, "I will remember that the next burden to be lifted from my drooping shoulders is the Nile." There is an aggressiveness, an undisguised contempt, a pitying patronage about the Superior Being who insists upon perennially sitting in Nile mud, and calling you from the antipodes to admire his poses, that makes you thirst for human blood. The greatest trial of Society is not being able to resent these underhand attacks upon one's self-esteem. It ought to be a criminal offence for any traveller to give his experience. "What is a prig?" asks Mrs. Vincy, in "Middlemarch." "A prig," replies her son Fred, "is one who makes you a present of his opinions." I am not a prig. I never make a present of my opinions. I am always paid for them.

I started for Biarritz, and did what must happen to every traveller at least once in his mad career. I arrived unknowingly at my destination, and was carried beyond it. Nobody told us where we were. This is a pleasant peculiarity of many Continental railroads, so that unless you are perpetually on the alert, and poking questions at the guard, you are kept on the rack. A party of Spaniards entered my compartment at a station which seemed to me very near Biarritz, and so interested me in their conversation about the war that my eternal vigilance — the price of safety in travelling — slumbered.

"You are going to Spain?" asked the agreeable Spaniard beside me, who spoke excellent English.

"No, to Biarritz."

"But you have gone too far. We have just left Biarritz."

I was frightened, and am not ashamed of the confession. Night had set in, a storm of wind and rain spread a wild gloom over a country of which I had no knowledge, and there was no return train until very late. Could I leave the train at the next stopping-place and take a carriage? The Spaniard thought it very likely, and out I got at a forlorn station standing alone in an uninhabited plain. Making my way through peasants of both sexes, I descried an open carriage at the back door. Would the driver take me to Biarritz? Well, he did n't know. He could n't for an hour, and he would n't for less than twenty francs.

"How many miles?"

"Nine."

I agreed to pay the amount asked, and off went driver and everybody else, including the station officials. Left in solitude, I imagined how easy it would be to rob me, quietly knock me on the head, and throw me into the Atlantic.

"Suppose the driver does not return?" I thought. But he came, and when he drove me off, with rain beating in my face, with wind howling in my ears, with restive horses and no lantern, I saw such an admirable opportunity for brigands and all the other horrors told in story-books, that I hardly enjoyed the novelty of the dramatic situation. At times the wind almost blew the light carriage over. Then I caught glimpses of the ocean, saw a revolving light flash red and white, and suddenly we came upon ox-teams creeping along, that frightened our horses into rearing and trying to run away. The driver swore whisperingly in choice Basque, and I wondered whether the friends who had promised to write neat obituaries would have an early opportunity of keeping their word. But no, my time had not come. I arrived alive at the hotel, and when I looked into the driver's face, which darkness had veiled, I beheld nothing worse than good-nature and shrewd honesty. "If you had screamed, we might have had our necks broken," was the only remark Monsieur le Cocher made on receiving payment and taking his departure.

The Superior Being who despises America and only consents to retain his nationality because he is indebted to it for fortune and the oppor-

tunity of associating with nobility, had told me
that Biarritz was the *beau idéal* of a watering-
place; that rain never fell there; and that comparing it with any spot in the United States
was akin to comparing Hyperion and Satyr.
"The blood of Douglas can protect itself," and
I do not feel called upon to annihilate every
American who displays his manhood by derid-
ing the beautiful and generous land of his birth;
but when I can prove him to be wanting in
veracity, I am so depraved as to rejoice. This
moral obliquity arises from an artistic sense of
symmetry. There should be harmony in nature, human or otherwise.

It rained at Biarritz as it rains in our own
South. Great big drops bombarded street and
roof, as though the clouds were waging a war
of extermination, and had ordered out their entire light infantry. Not content, it hailed, and
this was on the 15th of September. How moist

and uncomfortable it can be in the Pyrenees,
High and Low, can best be judged from the
eloquent fact that, in six weeks among the mountains and three days at Biarritz, I wore out a
pair of india-rubber overshoes. It was an era
in my life. I wrote lines to those overshoes,
and buried them — both lines and overshoes —
in the Atlantic, while the melancholy wind sang
a *miserere;* while the waves in their frenzy
dashed their white locks against the breakers,
and heaven itself shed tears.

So I saw Biarritz the beautiful under an umbrella. I saw it all in two hours, and longed
to give the Superior Being the benefit of my
observation. Biarritz is a small town of 3,652
souls, that twenty years ago was content to be
a fishing port, but since the Empress, in 1855,
built a big villa of English brick at the rate of
sixpence apiece, it has become the most fashionable seaside resort in France. Its climate, when

it does not blow and rain, is fine, and that it should be preferred to Boulogne, or other sea-ports, is not strange. Everything is compara-tive in this world, and Biarritz is worth a dozen Boulognes. In mud and rain I gazed upon white-washed lodging-houses, *cafés*, cottages, two big hotels, and a Casino, where everybody goes to meet everybody else, and read, or dance, or both. Dancing begins at 10 P. M., lasts until 3 or 4 A. M., when the Spanish women, who regulate manners, go to bed, with the intention of break-fasting the next afternoon. I went to the shore and asked to be shown the drive. There was none. I saw two good beaches and a pictu-resque cove, in the water of which women and children were jumping up and down under the protection of professional swimmers, the under-tow being so strong as to render bathing any-thing but a thoughtless amusement. I saw a few fine cliffs, forty or fifty feet high; I saw

rocks so porous as to have been eaten away by
the hungry sea. Thus are formed odd little
coves, into which the waves chase one another,
now in sport and now in anger; sometimes hug-
ging and kissing a promontory so persistently
that it wakes up in the morning to find itself
transformed into an island. I saw the square
Villa Eugénie looking like a hotel out of employment. I saw not a tree. I stood beside the
ruins of the old fort or lighthouse, l'Atalaye;
gazed over the turbulent expanse of the Bay
of Biscay; and, had the sun shone, I should have
seen the coast of Spain, with the peaks of distant Sierras rising behind it.

Here was a fine view, the one attraction of
Biarritz. After this survey I thought of Newport, with its charming harbor and dancing boats,
its graceful yachts and stately men-of-war; I
thought of Newport drives along the sea, and
Newport walks along the cliffs; I thought of

Paradise with its inviting shade, and Purgatory
with its frowning profile; I thought of Newport
bathing, soft and seductive as a woman in love;
I thought of Newport cottages and their many
charming inmates, and I said, then and there,
not Biarritz, Boulogne, Trouville, Brighton, Mar-
gate, and Ramsgate combined (and probably all
the other watering-places I have not seen), could
approach the varied beauty and comfort of Amer-
rica's Isle of Peace. Biarritz is good enough for
Europeans who have never visited Newport, and
for Superior Beings who are not fit to live in any
part of America whatsoever.

I had made a day's journey for the sake of
two hours' disillusion! It was humiliating. To
go through so much to get at so little! I would
be revenged. I would go to Spain and see Castelar. I would look a Carlist in the face and
ask him what century he was living in. I would
behold Spaniards on their native heath, discover

a Republican if possible, and to one and all I would propound the question, "What are you going to do about Cuba?" Then Biarritz would not be in vain. Warmed with expectation, I drippingly wended my way back to the hotel, and proclaimed my resolution. Friends shook their heads. Acquaintances looked at me in a dazed frame of mind, as though I had gleefully announced the day of my own funeral. "You will be shot by a chance bullet," said one. "You will be robbed!" exclaimed another: "all Carlists are brigands." Whereupon a very stormy-browed Spaniard looked over his paper and flashed lightning from his eye. He was a Carlist refugee, with neither the air of a brigand nor even that of a murderer. I merely saw Divine Right written upon his countenance. He had been born two hundred years later than his ideas. That was all. Nature seems to delight in bringing the centuries face to face that they may test

2

one another's strength by hand-to-hand fights.
She is determined that the Past shall be a thorn
in the flesh of the Present.

As usual, those persons were most prolific in
advice who knew nothing of what they were talking about. Had I been going up in the balloon
that accidentally did not cross the Atlantic Ocean,
I could not have been an object of greater com-
miseration. Unfortunately, advice is not always
information, and in all Biarritz there seemed to
be no one who could tell me the best route to
Spain. At last a handsome English captain,
who had been seven months with the Carlists in
the guise of correspondent, came to the rescue.
What did he think of them? He did n't think
of them. They were not worth thinking about.
They were a ragged lot of good-for-nothings, and
as for fighting in Spain, it was a farce.

" Do they postpone a battle on account of in-
clement weather ?" I asked.

"Well, yes, it is almost as bad as that. Don Carlos is a coward. He has n't slept since he crossed the frontier. There never was such a ridiculous war, and its continuance proves the weakness of the Madrid government. But the Carlists can't succeed, you know. They have neither money nor arms. I recently heard a French Legitimist bet one thousand francs that Don Carlos would be in Madrid in twelve months. The bet was taken by one of Don Carlos's own officers."

I told the handsome captain that I was on the point of going to Spain. Could he give me any advice? "Yes. Don't go." It seemed to him most extraordinary that a woman should want to do anything so excessively uncomfortable. Had he been American he would have sympathized with me at once. Being English, it took him fifteen minutes to get accustomed to the idea. At the end of that time he regretted his inability to accompany me to Madrid, for he said Spaniards were great brutes and had no consideration for women. But I must not go by land. The Carlists might detain me; they might confiscate the horses of the diligence and make themselves obnoxious in other ways. No, I certainly must go by sea, taking the good-sized steamer Diamant that left St. Jean de Luz for Santander three times a week.

Promising to follow the captain's instructions, I went in search of an American consul and a banker, both of which conveniences could only be found at Bayonne, six miles distant. To Bayonne I drove in the hood of a diligence, climbing to it by means of a ladder, and sitting for an hour with my feet in an ever-increasing stream of water, it being the peculiarity of a hood to keep the rain off one's head in order the more surely to submerge one's boots. This was discipline, I thought. This was the necessary preparation for a campaign in Spain. If I could go through water, I could go through fire. I do not now see the analogy between these two elements, but at the time my reasoning seemed incontrovertible.

Who was the American Consul? There was no Consul; but there was a Consular Agent. Our representative was a Frenchman who could not speak English. This appointment seemed as wise as most of our European appointments, and I wondered what seafaring men, who are not supposed to be linguists, did to make their wants known. There is probably an interpreter; but why give employment to men who are not sufficiently interested in their business to learn the language of the people they represent? It is not impossible to secure the services of English-speaking foreigners.

The Consular Agent would be back directly; would I wait? Sitting beneath the widespread wings of the American Eagle, I overheard a con-

versation between an elderly Englishman and a
Frenchman. The Englishman was a journalist.
" I 'm here in the interest of my paper," he observed, " but I 'm not to be lured into Spain.
'If you want your head to remain on your shoulders, you 'll keep out of Spain,' said the English
Consul, and he 's about right. Those Spaniards
are always cutting and slashing one another.
They never can be quiet. A good-for-nothing lot !
Why, they are worse than the French ! " This
was truly British, and the decorous silence that
followed was truly French. I envied the journal
that possessed a correspondent whose courage
was only equalled by his courtesy. At the close
of this remark, the Consular Agent appeared
upon the scene of inaction. Would he give me
a passport ? No, he would n't, for the excellent
reason that he could n't. Only ministers could
issue passports. Moreover, I had no need of a
passport. I was a woman. It was satisfactory to

be assured of my sex; nevertheless, in case of trouble, I wanted a certificate of American citizenship. Would the Consular Agent put that important fact down in writing, and stamp it with the seal of my country? The American Eagle almost flapped his wings and shrieked " E Pluribus Unum," in his desire to protect me from Legitimist brigands. More suspicious, the Consular Agent, who did not speak English, and could not tell an American by the horrible nasal twang which, according to Englishmen, is peculiar to this country (but which I know prevails in several English counties), looked at me, studied my letter of credit, and then good-naturedly complied with my request.

The Englishman who would not risk his precious life in Spain opened his mouth and eyes, and an elderly Frenchman followed me down stairs, making a profound bow as I entered the carriage. I was a heroine on such small

capital as to be ashamed of myself. I began
to feel as though I was drawing a hundred dollars' interest on an investment of fifty cents;
nor did the banker modify this sensation, for it
required quite twenty minutes to make him see
that a woman could go to Spain. After seeing
it, he entered into my plans with enthusiasm.
Money? That, of course. Courier I must have,
and he could secure one. In five minutes a
telegram sped to Biarritz for the purpose of
securing a man Friday. I shuddered at the
thought, for couriers are — couriers; but I did
not dare fly in the face of public opinion, especially in the face of a genial banker who spoke
English like a native, and took as much interest in my trip as though he had known me for
years. Anything he could do for me he would,
and I must write to him if I fell among thieves.
I left Bayonne feeling the richer by one new
friend.

With Spanish gold in my pocket I drove back
to Biarritz, and through the rain came he who
was to be my courier. With hat in hand he
stood before me, and my heart gave way at the
inspection. A short, fat man in slouchy clothes,
with a bullet head, small, blinking black eyes,
an inane mouth, and a weak chin. He was
flabby, mentally, morally, and physically; but
M. le Banquier certified to his honesty, which,
in a courier, is much. Then, he was considered
respectable. He was the father of a family. I
have known fathers of families who were not
respectable, but as tradition maintains the superiority of married over unmarried men, I do
not contradict it, whatever may be my private
opinion. The Flabby Blinker's smile in itself
was enough to exasperate one less susceptible
to human influences than myself. There was a
self-satisfaction and a patronage of all creation
about it that would have rasped an angel. The

idea of such human drivel being of any use to. an American was preposterous. Nevertheless, if anything happened, Society would say it was because I had obstinately refused to take a courier, so I stated my intentions. Did he speak Spanish? Had he any knowledge of Spain? The Blinker looked injured. Had he not lived twenty-six years in Spain, did he not speak the language like a native, and did he not know more about the people than they knew themselves? The Blinker assumed an air of importance that would have awed the entire Carlist army.

"Have no fear, madam; depend upon me, and you will see everything," exclaimed the Blinker.

"Very well," I said. "Go to Bayonne, get your passport, and be prepared to start in three hours."

The Blinker's jaw dropped. The Blinker said he could not get ready on such short notice; but on being told that, whether he could or could not, he must, he concluded to make a desperate effort, and actually succeeded in overcoming his own inertia. On his return, I said we would leave immediately for St. Jean de Luz, in order to take the steamer Diamant the next morning.

"Perfectly useless, madam," responded the Blinker. "No steamers have gone out for three days. The storm is not yet over, and the agents assure me there will be no departures for thirty-six hours at least."

I believed the Blinker. I did not then know, what experience has since taught me, that the thoroughly flabby temperament will never tell the truth unless bullied into it. To get at facts requires more effort than to draw on the imagination. The flabby temperament is not malicious; it is merely lazy; but the effect is the same. Every lie is founded on the text, how not to do it; the end and aim being never to do next week what can be postponed indefinitely.

PART II.

A Voyage to Santander.

II.

I WAS waked on the morning after finish-
ing my preparations for entering Spain,
by a sunbeam that danced upon my nose and
pried open my eyes. On leaving my room and
walking along the shore, I saw in the distance
a steamer. It had evidently sailed from St.
Jean de Luz. I knew then that I was the victim of misplaced confidence. I realized how Sam
Weller felt after having been trifled with by Job
Trotter. I decided who should command my
expedition into Spain. It was not the Blinker.

This booted boon made his appearance at noon,
carpet-bag in hand, from which he drew forth a
bottle of brandy and a bottle of wine. "The
wine is for me," he observed blandly. "You

"Nor do I like chickens rolled up in dirty newspapers."

never know what you are drinking in Spain."
(I had agreed to pay the Blinker's expenses.)
Then followed rolls of bread, sausages, and two
cooked chickens, done up separately in very inky

newspapers. I had desired the Blinker to pre-
pare a lunch for the steamer. He had done so
twenty-four hours too soon, adding insult to in-
jury by packing it in his bag.

"I never eat sausages," I said with dignity.

The Blinker smiled, and replied that it little
signified, as he ate them.

"Nor do I like chickens rolled up in dirty
newspapers."

The Blinker shrugged his shoulders, remark-
ing, "Que voulez-vous? One cannot always have
what one likes. I will eat one of the chickens."

I counted twenty and kept my temper.

"Look at the sun," I said.

"Yes ; a beautiful day for our journey," replied the Blinker unconcernedly.

"But you said it would rain. I have seen a
steamer depart that I am sure is the Diamant."

"Bien, madame. It does not rain. Tant

micux. The steamer you saw goes to Bilbao, not to Santander. We shall take Le Diamant to-morrow morning."

The glibness of the Blinker's tongue bore down my own conviction. There was an assurance in his statement that staggered me.

So we went by rail to St. Jean de Luz, the Blinker in a second-class carriage, I in a first-class carriage with all the impedimenta, and I asked myself what possible good or protection that lazy courier was to me. Did he assist me out of the carriage? No, indeed. I had performed a *pas seul* of great agility before discovering the Blinker struggling with his own legs that he had ingeniously contrived to get entangled with the carriage steps. He came up panting, and I then learned that whoever engages a fat courier will always be permitted to wait on himself, will always be late, and will always pay as much for porterage as though the courier were a prince imperial. Obesity in a courier is a crime.

While the Blinker was rescuing his legs from a predicament that no other legs could have invented, I made myself master of the situation and inquired about Le Diamant. Had it not sailed that morning with a swarm of Spanish refugees, who would not trust themselves in the small steamer, and would I not be obliged to wait several days for her return, as there were rumors of a quarantine at Santander?

"Do you hear?" I said, turning upon the Blinker. "The Diamant has gone, and I have lost twenty-four precious hours."

What difference did that make? A Phœnix could not rise half as quickly from his own ashes as the Blinker from his lies. He looked as innocent as a cherub. "Vraiment!" quoth he, "then we will await its return. I have lived twenty-six years in Spain —"

"We will not await her indefinite return," I replied, with a determination the Blinker had not before realized. "We will depart to-morrow, though we go to sea in a tub."

The Blinker again shrugged his shoulders, and we drove to Hotel de la Plage, before which the ocean is ever knocking, knocking, knocking, asking to be let in.

The day and view were lovely; the town was old, and, in spite of indignation, I could have been happy with a civilized companion; but with a human porpoise by my side, as gifted in expectoration as a Congressional lobbyist, how could I consider existence a blessing? I hoped that by some impossibility the Carlists would seize him and complete their ruin by putting him in command of a corporal's guard. Meanwhile it was my duty to see St. Jean de Luz, and I saw it. Having written harshly of Biarritz, I the more gladly testify to the exceeding superiority of its venerable neighbor. Had the Empress Eugénie possessed an artistic eye and a poetic soul, she would have revived the glories of St. Jean de Luz, rather than have founded the fashion of Biarritz ; but *parvenue* in all things, she preferred new whitewash to old wainscoting. Once a thriving port, sending vessels regularly to the whale-fishery, St. Jean de Luz now lives upon memories and — Spaniards. The former are permanent, the latter come with the bathing season, the French town being cleaner, and having better hotels, than have the Peninsula's seaside resorts. With a fine bay, a strong seawall, a large mole that adds as much beauty as safety to the port, with the river Nivelle, that for four miles is tidal and well adapted to boating, with pretty environs possessing far more shade than Biarritz, with several mountain excursions, St. Jean de Luz ought to be most popular. That it is not, only proves human subserviency to the dictates of a silly woman, who is all the sillier for being an Empress. Power frequently renders wise heads foolish, and weak heads mad.

The old town charms the artist by its quaint houses, arrayed in as many colors as Joseph's coat, with here queer gables, and there little coquettish balconies, over which lean buxom Spanish women, doing nothing in the world but languishing to the *andante* accompaniment of their fans. In the principal Place stands the Maison Lohobiague, or Château de Louis XIV., where the *Grande Monarque* stopped before and after his marriage with Maria Theresa, Infanta of Spain. Near by is the church in which the royal marriage was celebrated, only forty years after the landing of our Pilgrims, — a church externally grim and quaint, internally serving the Lord in very gaudy but shabby tinsel. Wherever I turned, in the old streets or the new,

I met young Spanish girls with expectation in their eyes, as though waiting for news from their fathers, brothers, or lovers, fighting the bad fight of Don Carlos, the Pretender. Some, forgetful, were riding donkeys that would not go; others were buying goats' milk of the old woman who kept her goats in the Place Louis XIV. Neither men nor women seemed to be borne down by the dissensions of their country, and I then and there decided to bear the woes of Spain with the equanimity of her own people. If they did not tear their hair, why should I? Perhaps one reason for not doing so is because they have so little. Spaniards are the most bald-headed of men and the most false-haired of women. Germany and the South of France adorn the civilized world with nature's capillary attraction, yet supply so fails to satisfy demand that erelong beauty may be reduced to the poet's line, and draw with but a single hair.

Was I not amused that day at dinner? The Blinker told me I should not have enough to eat unless he ordered a private table. I am not proud, if I am poor; and heretofore the table d'hôte had been sufficiently good. But when you travel with a courier, your first duty is to respect his feelings. Nothing degrades you so much in his eyes as the ignoble practice of economy. Couriers and economy assimilate about as readily as oil and water. While giving me instructions the Blinker looked as if to say, "Remember I 've a reputation to maintain, and if you disgrace me by sitting at table with other people, you will be sorry you were ever born." Not wishing to deplore my birth, I assented to his proposal. Ushered into the general dining-room, I was shown to a small table, while the other guests seated themselves at the long one. It startled me to see the Blinker place himself among them in a position where he could keep an eye on me. It was impossible not to admire his sublime coolness. He intended to eat, drink, and be merry at my expense, for to-morrow he would return to his own bread-and-cheese.

Nodding approvingly, as though my conduct so far were worthy of him, the Blinker led the conversation. "I have lived in Spain twenty-six years," he began. What followed I could not hear; but I remarked the perfect manners of the Spaniards, and contrasted them with English and Americans under a like infliction. The Blinker ought to have been thrown out of the window. His nearest neighbor was the Spaniard who had rescued me on the occasion of my being carried beyond Biarritz. The world is small. Be introduced to a man on the equator, and you will meet him at the poles. On my apologizing later to my rescuer for the Blinker's impudence, he replied: "I expect no more from people than they can give. I always know a frog

3   D

when I see it, though the creature endeavor to be an ox. Madam, your courier is a fool. In this he is not singular. Madam, he has sloven-ly manners. In these he is unique." After this concise prelude, we discussed Spain. "Madam," continued the Spaniard, " you will be disgusted, because you are an American, and will wonder why we talk so much and do so little. This is our habit, and it will take a long education to change what has become second nature. The Carlists are poor creatures, but the creatures of the Basque Provinces are poorer. They are as ignorant as ignorance ; they can neither read nor write ; the language they speak is not a written language ; they have no newspapers ; they are superstitious ; they are priest-ridden, and have been taught to consider Don Carlos a part of their religion. Don Carlos cannot succeed in ascend-ing the throne, but he can succeed in prolonging a civil war indefinitely. For myself, I belong to no party. Theoretically I believe in a republic, but the Spaniards are not republican. They are a brutal people, and too ignorant to know now what to do with liberty. Castelar is a pure man and a great orator, but he is not equal to the situation. I admire him, but do not believe in him. You will see. The Alphonsists are most likely to succeed. A constitutional monarchy is best suited to the requirements of Spain." Most astounding are these Spaniards. In one breath they proclaim themselves degraded beyond redemption; in the next they are the conquerors of the world, and who dare question their greatness? They are neither the one nor the other.

Out of respect to habit I went to bed that night, but the wild waves were putting so many questions to me that it was impossible to sleep, and at 2 A. M. a deep-voiced porter aroused me in a language I did not understand. The Basque dialect combines the vices of the French, Italian,

and Spanish, with no virtues whatever. To the
ear it is intolerable; to the understanding it is
incomprehensible. Not until recently have the
Basque schools been abolished, and not for another generation will the inhabitants of this province speak French. I made an elaborate toilet
by the light of the one candle for which the
plundered traveller pays a franc. Descending, I
found men and women sitting on trunks, munch-
ing dry bread, awaiting the omnibus that was to
convey us to the steamer. The Blinker was
drowning himself in coffee that he had consider-
ately ordered for me. I took none, because I
did not care to contribute more to the Atlantic
than absolutely became a woman who, the oftener
she goes to sea, the more she has reason to wish
herself on dry land. A horse knows perfectly
well when riders are afraid of him. Equally dis-
cerning is the ocean. Ever since I criticised the
Atlantic, it has resented my remarks in the most

underhanded manner. I knew how the Bay of Biscay would serve me, and prepared.

In rain, gloom, and darkness we groped our way to the omnibus that arrived an hour late. The steamer ought to have sailed before we left the hotel, and when I expressed concern, the proprietor stated that the steamer never started until it got ready, and when it got ready depended entirely upon circumstances. This was soothing information. Jog, jog, jog, went the omnibus through town, through suburbs, beside the sea, through muddy, dismal roads, with never a glimpse of the steamer, until everybody became nervous and hung more or less out of the windows. In moments of suspense, thrusting the head out of the window relieves the mind and seems to facilitate elucidation. It never occurred to the Spaniards to question the driver, and as I had hired a man to talk for me, I'd have died rather than have gratified my curiosity.

We overtook a lazier omnibus, and then we all breathed freely. I never before knew how much comfort could be extracted from the sight of an omnibus. At last we stopped on a long pier that did not seem to be in any business, but had moved out of town for the purpose of leading a quiet life and going fishing.

Landing in mud, we were surrounded by strapping young women, all clamoring for our trunks. In this remote spot women are porters, and men look on approvingly. The Blinker appeared to be an old acquaintance. "What, Jeannette," he said to a sturdy, good-looking, broad-shouldered girl, "you still here?"

"And, pray, why should n't I be?" she retorted.

"You ought to have been married, Jeannette."

"Married! Do you take me for a baby? Don't you know *I* know that marrying would only make matters worse, for then I 'd be obliged

to take care of two persons instead of one!
Now I am free and I can do as I like. Catch
me marrying!" After which Jeannette caught

"Catch me marrying!"

up my trunk as though it were a light basket,
balanced it on her head, and strode off swing-
ing her arms, laughing defiance to all men.

Amazed as I was at the civilization which turns women into men, I was delighted to note the physical strength of that score of girls. Jeannette could walk I don't know how many kilometres, with I don't know how many kilogrammes on her well-shaped head. All gave the lie direct to the miserable sentimental theory that women are born to be sickly dolls. If twenty Basque girls can rival men in endurance, millions of American girls can be made as healthy as they are beautiful; but this reformation will not come to pass in the days of hot-house rearing, heavy skirts, tight lacing, pointed heels, hot bread, and confectionery. Opponents of Women's Rights fear that, in obtaining political power, women will lose their charms. I have never found that treating women as intellectual, responsible beings deprived them of one iota of beauty or fascination; but I have always found that man's regarding woman as

his equal (if not superior) in physique, and
demanding from her the work of a horse, quickly
destroyed all symmetry of form. In the United
States, where women enjoy the greatest freedom,
they are the most feminine. Treated as though
possessed of man's muscle, without his brains,
the peasant women of Europe are the most
masculine of their sex. The right to labor without the right to think annihilates womanly inspiration. To transform women into beasts of
burden — only that and nothing more — is to
spoil one sex and travesty the other.

The Blinker entertained so great an admiration for the women porters that he entirely relieved himself of bundles. It was pure self-
sacrifice on his part, — and I paid for it. The
porters were paid for carrying our luggage to
the small boats plying between pier and steamer, somebody was paid for telling where we were
to sit, and the boatmen were paid for rowing.

3 *

The Blinker scolded, declared it an imposition, and then showered silver about with that generosity which invariably possesses people who spend the money of others. As we neared the steamer my desire to visit Spain was extremely slight. Had I been at Biarritz I should have found the best reasons for going north. The vessel, the Four Friends, bore a grimly humorous misnomer. I counted fifty passengers, and saw accommodations on deck for a dozen, and how we were to go on board was obscured in mystery. There was no ladder; the boat danced about as if it were over boiling water; the sailors screamed, flourished grappling-irons over our heads, and told us to swing ourselves on deck with a rope fastened at the steamer's side. Swing ourselves on deck! Did they take us for monkeys? A woman may be as agile as a fawn, and yet, in cumbrous clothing, display the awkwardness of an elephant. Then, too, a woman would rather part with her best friend than her dignity, and no dignity could swing over that horrible deck, which was so near and yet so far. O Spain, Spain, what crime did I not feel like committing in thy name! To have blown up the Four Friends would have settled the matter; but I only blew up the Blinker, who very nearly dropped me into the water, when, between climbing, leaping, and scrambling, I performed a series of gymnastics as difficult to conceive as they were to execute. The other women were hauled up by human derricks.

If, as Ruskin maintains, dirt be an element of the picturesque, the Four Friends would have thrilled him with delight. Had there been as much steamer as dirt, the Great Eastern would have had a dangerous rival. We walked over dirt, sat on it; and when I descended a steep, grimy ladder to inspect what

was courteously called the cabin, I saw a con-
tracted sty that none but human pigs could for
one moment have endured.   Compared with it,
the worst steamer crossing the English Channel
is Paradise.   The captain was a thin Spaniard,
with a dark, greasy complexion, dark, greasy
hair, nails and teeth in deep mourning, and a
short, bristling black beard, that made him look
like the first murderer in Macbeth.   The crew
were miracles of untidiness and deformity, the
most horrible of whom — a boy with one eye
and a deep gash in the place of the other —
performed the pleasing duties of steward with
the deftness of a hippopotamus.

"There is nothing like touching the world at
all points," I said to my disgusted self, as, enveloped in a waterproof, I curled up on the
least dirty bench to be found.   The rain pelted
upon the dilapidated awning drawn over the
deck, small streams finding their way down un-

suspecting backs and into helpless carpet-bags. There being few seats, men and women extended themselves upon the damp deck, and, embra-

"I curled up on the least dirty bench."

cing tin bowls, groaned in chorus as soon as the Four Friends weighed anchor. Everybody was sick, — everybody but the Blinker; nobody offered to assist anybody; several women

shrieked, several men howled, and one or two
rolled about in agony. The few French on
board suffered in silence. They never forgot to
be decent. Their neighbors could not remember
what they appeared never to have known.

In this pandemonium of dirt the greasy captain wandered about, talking at the rate of in-
calculable knots an hour. Had his tongue been
our motor power, we should have arrived at
Santander before leaving St. Jean de Luz. Unfortunately, it could be put to no such good use.
The captain merely succeeded in making us a
little more wretched than we otherwise should
have been. "I 'll do all I can for you! I 'll
do all I can for you!" he exclaimed, again and
again, in a superfluity of Spanish that would
have filled columns. "I 'll do all I can for
you; but I 'm greatly afraid I can do nothing.
In all probability we shall be detained in quarantine."

"In the name of common sense, why!" I asked, with a terror-stricken countenance.

"Well, you see, there is cholera in Paris."

"But we are not from Paris. There is not a passenger who is not from the South of France."

"It does n't make any difference," continued the voluble captain, who went from one to another, sawing the air, and diversifying the entertainment by flinging language at the ghastly-eyed steward-boy, and, during the flinging, drinking native wine that had a wonderful effect in enriching his vocabulary. From time to time the Blinker disappeared, returning with his mouth full, by which I knew he had been eating, in spite of his assurance that he was very ill, but had too much self-control to express his emotion. Finally the Blinker came to me with a small newspaper-bundle, saying that if I 'd eat a little I should feel better.

"Eat what?" I asked.

"Why, the chicken, of course; the chicken I cooked at Biarritz."

A stale chicken done up in newspaper, that for two days had been stowed away in the Blinker's carpet-bag. This was the delicacy offered to a deathly sea-sick woman!

"Throw that chicken overboard!" I gasped wildly.

"Bien, madame," replied the Blinker.

Would anything disconcert that exasperating courier? Overboard went the unprofitable chicken, and the sea made one mouthful of it. Had the Blinker and the captain gone after it, I should have felt better; but no, the Blinker patronized the universe with his smiling self-satisfaction, and the captain, who was his own perpetual encore, repeated quarantine variations. And to such an audience! In spite of their biliousness they were the right people in the right place. No dirt could shock them, nor wagging

tongue enrage. The entire cargo seemed to be
attacked by hydrophobia, shirts and pocket-hand-
kerchiefs having it in the most virulent form.
"Shall I too grow rabid," I asked my inner
self with horror, "here on the dreadful 'Bay
of Biscay O,' that terror of mariners about
which tenors sing sepulchrally?" My inner self
advised me to be calm, and, as the sun came
out when we steamed into the port of San Sebastiano, lighting up the lofty fort, burnishing
the waves, that, until then, had been a spiteful,
jealous green, it began to dawn upon me that
the world was not entirely composed of chop-
ping seas.

Nobody left the boat at San Sebastiano, and
several hydrophobiac patients came aboard. This
made bad worse; but, after attaining a certain
amount of misery, it matters little how much
more is inflicted. There are moral as well as
physical gymnastics. The athlete carries upon

his shoulders one, two, or three men with almost equal ease. Being able to carry the first man tells the training of the muscles. Bearing one mountain of misery denotes the capacity to endure Pelion piled upon Ossa. The additional hydrophobiac patients retired to the baggage, and roosted on the protruding ends of trunks. At least they roosted after we sailed. Prior to that, we underwent an infliction of custom-house officers. Why, no one could tell, as no one went ashore. Perhaps the officers needed a little relaxation. The mere fact of there being no reason for doing a thing appears to be the very best reason — in Spain — why it should be done at all hazards.

But no filthy steamer, no Spaniard, can destroy the interest of the Spanish coast. In solitary beauty, — almost as lifeless as when the world began, — the Spanish Pyrenees, massed against the sky, surge along the coast in loftier,

grander billows than any that the ocean invokes.
Cruel as they are beautiful, they excite fear while
extorting admiration, for harbors are few and the
mariner knows but too well what dangers lurk
at their feet. Playing hide and seek on their
dimpled, many-colored sides, the sun makes
charming pictures for a brilliant colorist, yet an
artist of sensibility would lose heart, for what is
more chilling than inhospitable beauty? "You
are very fine," I said. "I am glad I have seen
you, but you are treacherous. Even in sunlight
you dazzle without warming, and even in good
weather I would not be at your mercy. If you
dumbly indicate the character of the people
whose northern coast you defend so successfully,
then shall I be as glad to see the last of them
as I am to see the last of you."

The last, however, was long in coming. Not
until eight in the evening did we creep up the
beautiful harbor of Santander, welcomed by the

twinkling lights of piers and vessels, and so long
undisturbed in our progress that we began to
think the captain's quarantine ravings as mythi-
cal as Spanish unity. I was picturing a comfortable supper in a comfortable room, the floor
of which had no tendency to turn upside down,
when the Four Friends suddenly stopped. Did
it mean quarantine? The captain's arms flew
round like a windmill in a hurricane, but with
no benefit to our curiosity. Finally, a long-boat
came to us, and a man with a lantern talked to
our captain, who, on being asked for a list of the
passengers, could not give it. Had he not given
one list to the authorities at San Sebastiano? And
how could he make out another when there was
nothing to be done? Below he went, and there
we sat, famished, cold, damp, weary, waiting for
what ought to have been ready at once. "Was
it quarantine or not?" we asked, as the boat
pushed off. "Quien sabe!" There we brooded

another hour before official word came. Yes, we were doomed to quarantine. But when and how much of us? Again the boat disappeared, and we sat in moist darkness until the clock struck ten. I had prepared for bandits, Carlists, and stray bullets, not petty annoyances, the endurance of which is no heroism, and the relation of which makes no particular hair stand on end. That going to Spain in war-time should be very like a lecturing tour in my own enlightened country — only worse — struck me as, to say the least, unromantic.

Upon the return of the officials, we were told to go ashore with ourselves and our hand-bags, but to leave all trunks on board. Thankful for release on any terms, we dropped ourselves into long-boats, put our feet into unseen pools of water, and were rowed to the nearest pier, where men with torches were shouting about nothing, as usual, and women, that might as well have

been men, shrieked for the right to take our
money by carrying our bags. The Blinker paid
the rowers, then paid a woman for hauling him
up the pier, then paid another woman for ex-
tending the same civility to me, then he engaged
boys to carry what he ought to have carried
himself, and then we went in search of a lodging. The night was beautiful. All Santander
swarmed upon the quay, which is the principal
business street, and many a curious glance
greeted us as we wandered from hotel to hotel.
Refugees had taken possession of every place,
and it was not until after recourse to eloquence
that a French *maître d'hôtel* gazed upon me com-
passionately, and found a room, previously swear-
ing to a dozen other travellers that if his own
grandmother had descended from heaven to
pass the night at Santander, he could offer her
no more generous hospitality than a peg on
which to hang herself. "I am very grateful to

you for treating me better than your revered
grandmother," I said, when the *chef* showed me
to a forlornly thin, tall room.

"Madam, I never liked my grandmother!"

"Madam," replied the *chef*, "I never liked
my grandmother," and, with a bow, retired.

PART III.

From Santander to Madrid.

4

III.

An Episode of Spanish Quarantine. — Fumigating an Empty
Trunk. — The Blinker every Inch Himself. — Incidents of
Railroad Travelling.

SPAIN acquaints one with strange bed-
fellows. There is an untiring industry
about them worthy of a better cause. Would
that the Republic's Minister of Finance and
its commanding generals possessed the activity
of its fleas! Why will Nature be such a spend-
thrift? Were she to economize on fleas, there
might be sufficient energy in the Peninsula to
start the trains punctually and occasionally turn
promises into deeds. Why there should be so
many Spanish fleas weird William Blake would

quickly tell us. When completing his curious drawing of the Ghost of a Flea, the lively ghost informed Blake that all fleas were inhabited by the souls of such men as were by nature blood-thirsty to excess, and were therefore providentially confined to the size and form of insects. With this strange light thrown upon Spain's largest population, it is most wasteful management that fails to utilize fleas for war purposes. Placed at the head of the army, they would soon drive the Carlists howling into the Bay of Biscay.

I doubt whether the Blinker's repose were more tranquil than my own, for at an early hour he informed me through the keyhole that orders had been issued to detain the luggage of the Four Friends three days in quarantine. "So, madam, we must remain here for your trunk. My carpet-bag has been given up."

"Three days! Never. Three hours. We will

take the train that goes to Madrid at 2 P. M.
Meanwhile, we will go to the health authorities
and demand my property."

The Blinker muttered something in opposition.
He always was in opposition. He contradicted
by impulse. That a woman, not yet a grandmother, should have " views," seemed to him
revolutionary. Off we tramped at nine o'clock,
without breakfast, with a small beggar to show
us the route. He was an independent beggar.
Though politely requested to make haste, our
ragged cicerone sauntered, regardless of his fol-
lowers, who were somewhat amazed when he suddenly disappeared. Where had he gone ? Into
a shop to buy some paper with which to make
a cigarette that, on his return, he slowly puffed
in our faces. It struck me as the coolest performance at which I had ever assisted. It also
struck me as the solution to several Spanish
problems.

Santander is not a big town, otherwise we might be wandering about to this hour. When cigarettes are to be smoked with tender appreciation, distances become great; but we found the sanitary bureau and harangued the mighty potentate thereof. I was an American whose stay in Spain was limited to a few days. Could I have my trunk?

"No."

"Why not?"

"Because there is cholera in Paris?"

"But I've not come from Paris, nor have any other passengers."

"It matters little. We are held responsible for the introduction of cholera into Spain, and every province exercises its own discretion in this matter."

"Where is the logic or discretion of allowing passengers to land with all such luggage as can be carried by hand, and only retaining trunks

for fumigation? Is the cholera locked up in my
trunk and not in my courier's carpet-bag? Had
I known the marvels of Spanish quarantine, I'd
have brought my clothes in a newspaper."

The potentate heeded neither argument nor
sarcasm. He smoked a cigarette, and seemed
perfectly resigned to my fate. I wrestled with
the Spanish intellect. I tried to make him realize that the eyes of Europe and America would
be everlastingly fixed upon him if he forced me
to go to Madrid with one gown. At this final
threat the potentate relented. " You cannot
have your trunk," he said. " That would cost
me my office, but I will give you such a paper
as will enable you to take out its entire contents." And the potentate gave me a written
order addressed to the quarantine officers. To
the last he did not seem to appreciate the absurdity of persecuting my innocent trunk.

Thanking the potentate, we went in search of

banker and American Consul, as it seemed to me that such a ridiculous law might be overruled by powerful influence. The Spanish banker received me with stately dignity, looked at my letter of credit, heard my pathetic story, and said he could do nothing. Law was law. This, from a native of the country that makes more laws and fulfils fewer than any nation in the world, impressed me. We bade each other farewell with profound bows, and soon I stood in the small office of the American Consulate. Of course the Consul was a Spaniard who could not speak English ; but I am assured that he is efficient, and that his assistant understands our language. Half a dozen men were smoking, all of whom stopped puffing as the thrilling tale was told. They examined the order, and then the Consul said : " Madam, I don't know how you have obtained this document, but you are given extraordinary privileges. No human being can obtain more. Take your clothes, and I will send the trunk back to Bayonne." There was no power behind the Consul. The telegraph-wire to Madrid was cut, and I gave up the contest. Then I fell to questioning. What did the mercantile community think of Castelar?

"A great orator, a good man, one who would do everything for Spain if he could, but he cannot. He lacks executive force. He is a dreamer, not a statesman."

"What are the chances of a republic?"

"They are small. We have a republic without republicans. We are opposed to Carlism. We want peace, and will accept whatever gives it to us."

With this confession of faith ringing in my ears, we left the Consulate.

What next was to be done? To go in search of the Four Friends. And where was it? In the neighborhood of quarantine? And where

4 *

was quarantine? Across the harbor, five miles away. It was half past ten o'clock, and the Madrid train started at two. How long would it take to go and return? About two hours, if nothing happened. As something always happens when one is in a hurry, I begged the Blinker to secure the lightest boat and strongest rowers. He smiled, went to the quay, returned, and escorted me to a heavy tub commanded by an old man and manned by a small boy. I said nothing. Of what use? The Blinker would have assured me that the boat was the best in the harbor. "Now, my good friends, hurry. · I 've no time to lose," I exclaimed. Whereupon man and boy sat down to indulge in a dialogue as to whether they should or should not carry a sail. Deciding affirmatively, the boy went in search of one, and in the course of twenty minutes the unwieldy thing was in place. "Now we are off," I thought. No, we were not. Then began the

most important **work of the day**, — making cigarettes. The entire Spanish nation begins and
ends in smoke. **With the first puff** we were
under way so far as concerned the sailing ; but,
as the wind was very **light, I** suggested rowing. Would **the noble, independent** Spaniards
row ? No ; they preferred **smoking** and conversation. **Why should they wear** themselves out ?
The sea glittered like molten silver, the air was
soft, the sky beautiful. **Why exert the** muscles ?
To talk about being in **haste seemed to them** an
evidence of insanity.

As man and **boy sat puffing, puffing,** puffing, I
wondered **whether the former** had any political
opinions, whether **the condition of Spain** interested him. He looked **lazy and ignorant** enough
to be a Carlist, and I asked him if he were so.
For the first time a slight gleam · came into his
eyes.

"Carlist ? No. If Don Carlos succeeds, the

Inquisition will be revived within twenty-four hours. We don't want the Inquisition. When the authorities came to me, I said I was a republican, and I put my cross on a piece of paper that they told me signified my allegiance to the government. I am a republican because under a republic commerce will flourish and living will be cheaper. I can wear better clothes and have more of them."

It was not the most enlightened republicanism I had ever dreamed of, but it was so much better than Carlism that I felt a certain amount of sympathy for the speaker, who gradually became interested in my fate and evinced a slight desire to get over the water. When we arrived at quarantine the Four Friends was spluttering and shrieking, backing and filling, trying to effect a landing. Heeding our pantomime, she stopped, and by a repetition of the gymnastics practised on a more formidable occasion, I went aboard.

The quarantine officer looked at the order, said it was queer, but that there was nothing to prevent my emptying the trunk inside out. This I knew, and in five minutes we jumped into our boat with the biggest, absurdest-looking bundle I ever saw in the possession of any one not an emigrant. It was half past twelve o'clock. Both current and wind were against us, and I began to despair. Would the good men row? Well, yes, they would. They did not want me to be left by the train. And they dipped their oars into the water with something akin to vigor. It was not what I call rowing, but I had begun to grow reasonable, and not to expect Yankee energy from Spanish lazzaroni. Slowly we approached the town, the wind helping us on the last tack. What time was it when we landed?

"Eight minutes past two," said the Blinker's watch.

"Ten minutes before two," said mine.

The Blinker declared his time was precisely that of the cathedral, and it was useless to think of catching the Madrid train. I said that, according to the church clocks in the morning, my watch was right. The captain and crew would not commit themselves to either side, and I silenced the Blinker by telling him to do as I said and not say what I should do. He smiled, of course, and with a beggar running in advance, carrying my ridiculous bundle on his head, for which I felt an apology was due to the gaping multitude, we strode into the hotel. Where was the station? Near by. Where was a carriage? None to be had. Everybody walked. Should I be in time for the train? My friend the *maître d'hôtel* did not know. I could but try. The Blinker disappeared. I cried aloud for more beggars. They swarmed. To my room I rushed, collected more bundles, consigned them to my small army, paid the hotel bill, and then looked about for the Blinker. The *maître d'hôtel* rushed up stairs after my enterprising courier.

"Where is your carpet-bag?" I asked.

"O, are you really going?" he exclaimed, retiring, and returning with his luggage. "Good by," he said blandly to the *maître d'hôtel.* "We'll be back directly."

Beggar.　　Beggar.　　Beggar.　　Myself.　　The Blinker.

Was not this insulting? Was it not enough to make an American perform a war-dance? In single file we hurried to the station. We did not run ; I found it impossible to run in Spain. And what o'clock do you suppose it was when we arrived? Charming diversity of time! Ten minutes before two! I did n't make a speech to the Blinker. With a deportment worthy of the noble soil beneath my feet, I merely pointed to the clock and said, " I told you so."

The Blinker smiled.

Such a crowd! It seemed as though half the world had assembled on the platform to bid an everlasting farewell to the other half huddled together in the train. I felt somewhat like a victim, as going to Madrid was not the safe journey it had been. An accident had occurred not many days before, the sum total of which was seventeen killed and several wounded. Some maintained it to have been the result of a Carlist conspiracy ; others blamed the road. Nobody knew, and I trusted to about all one can trust, — luck. Every place was occupied but a coupé, into which I climbed, — for that is what entering a European railway-carriage means, — the beggars and the Blinker barricading me with bundles. I have always had a contempt for women who travel with bundles. Bundles are but one remove from bandboxes. And here was I with the contents of a trunk in my arms! Of course everybody's eyes were fastened on that blue-and-white checkered bundle, — done up in a morning wrapper, — and of course I could not rise to explain. I sympathized with Pickwick and his sporting friends when they went about all day with a dreadful horse which they could not rid themselves of and were accused of stealing. I wanted to put my head out of the window and assure people I was not a receiver of stolen goods.

We departed at twenty minutes past two! Hereafter I shall never despair of catching a Spanish train, for, although it may have started,

I shall be sure to catch up with it by walking over the track, because it stands still much more than it goes ahead. Why trains should stop at any way-station seems curious, nobody appearing to enter or leave them. Whenever the train for Madrid did stop, however, I concluded it was for the night. I believe the cause of detention is due to tobacco, — heaven's last, best gift to man. At every station engineer, firemen, all, make cigarettes, and do not start until the last puff has been drawn. Time was made for slaves. Are Spaniards slaves? They are the cause of slavery in others.

Converting my checkered bundle into a pillow, I congratulated myself on having a coupé wherein to be moderately comfortable. I had had nothing to eat for two days except a few grapes; but it is astonishing how one can live without eating after becoming accustomed to it. Was I allowed to remain in peace? Certainly not.

While we were fondly lingering at a station not many miles from Santander, a young man opened the door and politely asked me if I had a coupé ticket.

"No; I saw the coupé empty. No official could or would give me any information about it, and I got in."

"There are others who wish the coupé."

"Possession is nine points of the law."

"Certainly, madam, but there are three gentlemen who wish to occupy the other seats, and unless you take the compartment they have a right to them."

"Are they Spaniards?"

"Yes, madam."

"Do they smoke?"

"Certainly, madam."

"It is impossible. I can't endure smoke all night. There is no compartment for women. I must take the coupé."

"But, madam, you will ruin yourself. The coupé will cost you a great deal of money."

"How much?"

The polite young man sat down and did sums for ten minutes, at the end of which time he presented a bill that staggered my intellect and frightened my purse. In all my experience I had never known such extortion.

"What does this mean?"

"It means that the government taxes railroads to such a degree as to put up fares. I thought you did not know Spain. It really will not pay you to take this coupé. At —— a carriage with compartment for *Dames Seules* will be put on, and then I advise you to change. Until then you can have the coupé to yourself."

Such interest in my pocket touched me. How did that unknown young man divine my financial status? Why did he not take me for an "American Princess"? Was it being without a trunk, travelling with a steerage bundle, that revealed my abject squalor? Yes, a woman is known by her trunks. I did not inform my economical friend that I owned a courier. I was so glad to be rid of the Blinker that I would not have called for his assistance had my bundle been borne off by brigands. Upon arriving at ———, true to his word, the polite young man appeared with porters, escorted me and my bundles to a woman's compartment, and bade me a good night.

On general principles I object to the compartment for *Dames Seules :* first, because *Dames Seules* usually carry as many bundles as I did on this exceptional occasion, and stow them away in the places where legs ought to go; second, because they travel with babies that cry, or small children that eat candy or cake and then wipe their dear, dirty little fingers on your new travelling-gown; third, because they have as much

as they can do to take care of themselves, and
never volunteer to help you in or out of the carriage, or fetch you a glass of water, or say civil
things to you. I always avoid *Dames Seules*, but
in Spain I was grateful for them. On entering, I
beheld three ladies and two children. They were
exceedingly courteous, gave me two seats and
fastened their black eyes on my bundle. To vin-
dicate my right to respectability, I told them the
story of the quarantine. They listened gravely,
never dreamed of smiling, and merely remarked
that I was very brave to come to Spain at such
a time. "But," they added, "American women
are not like European. They travel about like
men. It must be very fatiguing, and to come
to Spain! After seeing Paris, what is there in
Madrid, especially now?"

"You are not republicans?"

"O no; nor any one else," replied the most
voluble of the señoras.

"Are you in favor of Don Carlos?"

"Not at all. It is a great trial to be torn to pieces by civil war, but we are obliged to endure it. The best Spaniards are Alphonsists. The Queen we do not want. She has disgraced us; but her son is our legitimate sovereign. Unfortunately, he is very young. We fear a regency, and so accept the present government."

"Then you regard the republic as a *pis-aller*."

"Precisely."

"What do you think of Castelar?"

"He is a good man and a fine orator; but he can never accomplish what he has undertaken. We are biding our time."

Poor Castelar! How I pitied him! Atlas bearing the earth on his shoulders had no such burden. The farther I got into Spain, the farther off seemed the republic.

"Dinner! dinner! twenty minutes for dinner!" and off everybody rushed to the dining-

room of a restaurant. It was the only occasion
on which I saw Spaniards in a hurry, although
Gautier declares that they are the greatest walk-
ers and most agile runners. They would have
done credit to a Western steamboat, as described
by Dickens thirty years ago. I had succeeded
so well without eating, that to dine seemed like
throwing away money. However, early prejudices
still clung to me, and I sat down beside a nice-
looking Spanish woman, who immediately began
to talk broken English. It really is provoking
not to be able to pass for somebody else occasionally, but the Anglo-Saxon is so branded with
national characteristics as to render concealment
impossible. This woman ate; I could not. There
came soup with oil in it; then dry fish with oil
on it, followed by pork and oil. I fell back on
a bit of done-to-death beef and underdone potato.
At least I made the effort, but had no knife.

"Bring me a knife," I said to a waiter laden
with dishes.

"Certainly," said the waiter, and never returned.

"Bring madam a knife," said the Spanish woman to another waiter.

"Certainly," he replied, and never returned.

Both, probably, came back the next day. The one word in everybody's mouth is *mañana* (to-morrow). It appears to be the appropriate answer to any question, and has so taken possession of the Spanish mind that I don't believe Castelar himself would dare to do to-day what he could put off until to-morrow. It was not feasible to postpone my dinner, so I poised my beef on the point of a fork and gnawed it, to the amazement of some old Spaniards opposite, who picked their teeth in chorus, and glared. Said they, probably, when seated smoking in a hermetically sealed compartment, "What queer people are the English! They never use a knife. They stick their meat on a fork, and bite around it." I did n't like gnawing, and, after deferring to my stomach by indulging in several mouthfuls, I arose. The somewhat distant Blinker, who was seated at the same table devouring all within his reach, also rose, smiled upon me, and signified in porpoise-like pantomime that he would pay for my dinner. The benevolence and oil beaming on that man's face deserved to be immortalized by John Leech. He was a leech, but not John.

It is a long night that has no morrow. Long as it was, the end came before I died for want of fresh air. Thinking me asleep, my neighbors stole to the window and closed it, counted their beads, and said their prayers in unison. The sound was like the hum of bees. Then the ladies removed their bonnets, took off their hair, tied their remains up in silk handkerchiefs, and I watched them, nod, nod, nodding, until daylight.

The view within did not excite, nor did that without. When Dickens wishes to describe deso-

lation, he says, "Few children were to be seen,
and no dogs." Had he visited Spain, he would
have drawn a picture of naked, russet mountains,
stretching north and south, east and west, staring
out of an atmosphere so clear and thin as to render their bleak monotony all the more startling,

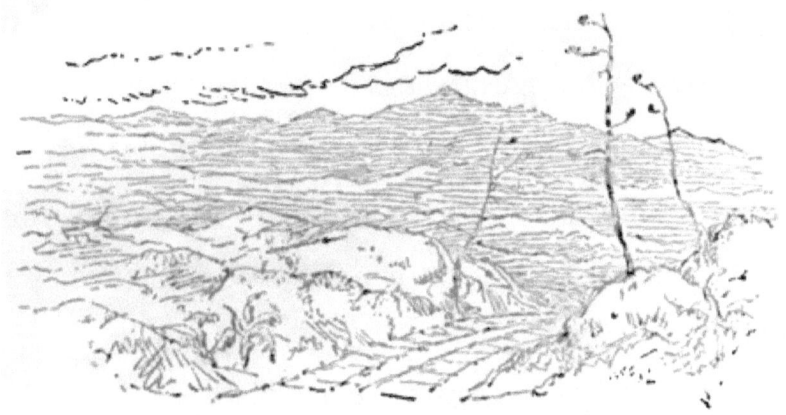

Naked, russet mountains,—all dead but the train.

without cultivation, without habitation, saving
here and there the wretched ruin of a wretched
stone sty, in which once may have wallowed
mediæval beggars, giving no hope for either time
or eternity. I became more and more oppressed
by the absence of life. That a railroad track

should be laid down in such a region, that a train should be slowly climbing an inclined plane, that occasional dreary stations, seemingly attached to no town, should punctuate our progress, seemed a ghastly joke; and when, early in the morning, we passed the Escorial, built high in the air, and starting out of the solitude like the great grim parody on humanity that it is, I saw in its gridiron the bier of past and present Spain. This is the country that once ruled the world, the country to which America owes its discovery!

Is anything as incredible as history?

PART IV.

Madrid.

IV.

First Impressions of the City. — A Bull-Fight. — The Sanguinary Instincts of the Spaniards. — Cock-Fighting. — Spanish Cooking.

WITHOUT the customary warning of environs, without premonitions of human existence, I found myself shot into the capital of Spain, which seems to have been dropped into the middle of a plain twenty-four hundred feet above the level of the sea, for no better reason than incongruity. The eternal fitness of things did not preside over the founding of Madrid. How could it? Idiocy is the divine right of kings. "I doubt," writes Irving, "if the king who first made Madrid a court residence has yet got out of purgatory, for this monstrous evil inflicted upon the nation and its visitors." The dirty station looked as though it had been put up temporarily the night before, and did n't intend to be of any more use than it could help. The day being a festival, crowds of peasants stood about waiting to go into the country, — going into the country meaning visiting the Escorial and ruminating over the bones of brutal Philip the Second. They could not go in search of trees, because there are none. Third-class passengers, packed like sardines, howled as they departed, and addressed the multitude in doubtful Castilian. At first I thought they were organizing a revolution, but I soon discovered that they were merely insulting lookers-on.

Hurrying away, we were driven to the Hotel de Paris, in the Puerta del Sol, a square which is as much the centre of Madrid as Madrid is the centre of Spain. All roads lead to it; and what does not happen there is not worth happening

at all. Sit in the café under the Hotel de Paris,
and Spain will revolve around you, particularly
at 2 o'clock in the morning. Then citizens begin
to feel the enlivening effects of countless cigarettes and innumerable glasses of sweetened water. Madrid goes to bed at 3 A. M., breakfasts
at 1 P. M., takes a siesta before going to the bull-
fight at 4, drives afterward, dines at 7, and later
begins business. There are those abject enough
to retire at night and rise in the morning. They
are shopkeepers and secretaries of legation possessed of conscience. Conscience emulates the
lark. It rises early.

I was in Madrid, eating a real breakfast, thousands of miles from home, and not knowing a
soul. What had I come for? To look Spain in
the face, and see Castelar. As I ate I pondered,
and as I pondered I ate. A handsome Italian
garzone stood by, and we discussed Spain in *la
lingua del sì*. The hotel — the best in the coun-

try — is kept by an Italian, and his most faith-
ful servants are countrymen. What did the *garzone* think of the republic?

"Ah, Signora, what would you? The Spaniards are ignorant and cruel. They are not republican. Nobody that I see wants a republic.
Everybody wants something else; but, as all are
quarrelling among themselves, Señor Castelar
maintains his position. He is a good man. He
writes fine books, and makes beautiful speeches.
But the end of it will be that we shall have a
king. I am sick of it all, and I 'd like to go
to America, where people are intelligent and the
poor have a chance to rise."

This was at 11 o'clock in the morning, when
I wondered what should be done first. Four
hours later, all the rough places were smoothed
out by kind Americans. To discover people is
far more delightful than to discover things. If
more money were spent on human and less on

geographical explorations, the world would be a deal happier. What sympathy can you extract from the North Pole or the sources of the Nile? Both throw cold water on you. My discoveries are entirely confined to people; and because of such a discovery, five hours after breakfast I was driven to a bull-fight. I ought not to mention the fact; I ought to have been too virtuous to go. But as American clergymen visiting Spain always attend bull-fights, making the self-sacrifice in order to warn their flocks against them, I had no scruples. I might assert that I was actuated by the noblest motives; but I think my real reasons were curiosity and a desire to see Spain in her glory. If her glory be that of the slaughter-house, to the slaughter-house will I go — once.

It was the feast of Our Lady of Sorrows. What more fitting than a bull-fight? Everybody by the name of Dolores, and everybody by any other name less bitter, filled the sunny

streets, all hastening, as much as their nationality would permit, in one direction. There was
a startling unanimity of opinion. There were no
two ways about it. If the Spaniards could only
agree as cordially about a government as they
do about a bull-fight, the world would gaze upon
such a happy family as never yet roared in a
menagerie. Alas! unanimity among Spaniards
means butchery — either of horses, bulls, Cuban
students, or Cuban patriots. The taste of the
Inquisition still remains in their mouths.

Making our way through the human hive
swarming in the Puerta del Sol, down the Calle
de Alcala, across the Prado, deserted even by
dogs, through the Puerta de Alcala, we slowly
drove, and stopped at the Plaza de Toros. We
were welcomed by a regiment of beggars, — all
in their holiday dirt, the women bearing their
holiday babies, — ready to hold the horses, open
doors that did not need to be opened, show us

to our entrance, relieve us of our pocket-books, and pray for our salvation. I saw more interesting cases for surgical operations than gladden professional eyes in American hospitals from one year's end to another. I saw more filthy children being trained up in the way they should not go — to a bull-fight or anywhere else — than would have supplied a ragged-school.

But enough of beggars is as good as a feast of office-seekers, and we finally succeeded in mounting very rickety stairs and seating ourselves in a box excellent for sight and sound. We were three, — a Rhode-Islander, a New-Yorker, and, it may be superfluous to add, myself. I felt proud of my company. They did credit to their country and their sex. Their sex was not mine. If the eyes of America had fallen upon them, she might have exclaimed, as did Cornelia under similar circumstances, "These are my jewels." First, I saw a great wooden circus open to the sky, with one row of boxes above, an amphitheatre below, and an immense ring separated from the amphitheatre by a red barrier six feet high, called *las tablas,* and an alley about five feet wide. Then I saw 14,000 Spaniards, the men wearing civilized trousers and chimney-pots, the women occasionally varying bonnets with mantillas. There was no effect of color, saving such as was produced by the waving of cheap and badly tinted fans in that part of the circle exposed to a blazing sun. Everybody appeared excited, and cries of "Agua, agua!" added to the pandemonium. The Spanish thirst for blood is diluted in water, — a most unusual European beverage. Perhaps Spaniards steep themselves in water because there is so little of it in the country. Human nature is born perverse. Thanks to that wise forethought which has cut down all the trees, and consequently dried up most of the streams, Spain is as arid as America will be, if the present suicidal, forest-destroying policy is pursued two or three centuries longer.

Next, I heard a wretched band play wretched music. Then began the procession of the *dramatis personæ*, who marched round once and disappeared. The play consists of three acts. In the first, the horses are killed; in the second, the bull is worried and wounded; in the third, the bull is killed. To every performance there are six plays, in which six bulls and at least twenty-four horses are slaughtered. So you perceive how busy Mr. Bergh would be if he lived in Spain and there were a society for the prevention of cruelty to animals. But there is n't, and there will not be for fifty years. I remember, once upon a time, assisting at an Italian spectacle wherein Frances Power Cobbe expostulated with a driver for beating his overworked horse. He looked at her with amazement, and exclaimed, "Ma signora, non è Cristiano!" (But, madam, he is not a Christian!) Latin races have no more feeling for animals than the Inquisition had for heretics. Beasts are not Christians. They have no souls to be saved. And of all the Latin races, Spaniards are the cruelest, because, I suppose, they spring from the fiercest blood and are the most ignorant. Ignorance is the worst of enemies.

If the men were killed in bull-fights, I should say nothing more than " it serves them right." But, with the usual amount of justice meted out in this calculating world, they alone escape. Rarely are men injured in the ring. Skill and precaution save them ; unsuspecting hacks, blinded on the side presented to their powerful opponent, and bulls that have never been warned of their doom, are gored and butchered amid a multitude of human yells. If by a miracle a man loses his life, his soul is saved ; for have not bull-fighters their private chapel at the entrance to the ring, and is there not a priest in readiness to absolve them?

There is a deal of fiction about a bull-fight. The two *alguacils* on horseback, who, clothed in black, headed the procession, exhibited two handkerchiefs apiece, peering from pockets on their breasts. Why, no one remembers. An alguacil began Act First by dashing up to the box of the President, from whom he received the key of the gate at which the bulls entered. Was the gate locked? No. The alguacil rode back to the gate, it was thrown open, and out rushed a brown and white bull, wearing the colors of the hidalgo on whose farm he had been bred. The bulls for Our Lady of Sorrows were raised by a noble duke, a lineal descendant of America's discoverer, bearing his honored name, Cristobal Colön. Whether the human stock has degenerated in its pursuits is a matter of taste. We prefer America to bull-fights; Spaniards prefer bull-

fights to America. But Christopher Columbus
raises fine bulls; there are none better.

With a trumpet-blast the "lord of lowing
herds" dashed into the ring. For two days he
had been kept in the dark without food. Fancy
then his bewilderment and rage when, blinded
by the sun, and excited by the screams of 14,000
throats, to the left of the gate, which closed immediately, he saw a *picador* dressed in yellow,
wearing a broad-brimmed hat, mounted on a sorry
beast, and holding in his right hand a threaten-
ing lance. Could anything have been more inviting to bullish instinct? In one moment, the
bull's horns penetrated the horse's bowels, and
the lance was plunged into the bull's back. The
bull was game; he showed unusual pluck, and
the Spaniards cheered. Again and again he returned to the charge. There never was a better
bull. He lifted the helpless horse off his feet;
he almost carried him on his horns; he no more

heeded the lance than if it had been the prick-
ing of a pin; he gored and gored until the
wretched horse, quivering from head to feet,

Rescuing the Picador.

silently fell to the ground with the picador beneath him. The man was in no danger. The
bull's attention was quickly distracted by the
waving of red banners in another direction, and

assistants rescued the picador, whose high tournament saddle prevented him from being easily thrown, and whose legs were so cased in iron as to render it impossible for him to move until set upon his feet. On the picador's removal the teasing ceased, and the bull, seeing the dead horse bathed in his own blood, charged him many times amid popular bravos. Descrying another horse, off the bull dashed with his hoofs in the air, and so nearly tossed his victim as to unhorse the picador, who clung to the barrier until hauled over it. The horse galloped riderless round the ring with his bowels dragging upon the ground. It was a noble sight. Perhaps you think the suffering brutes are speedily put out of misery. You are wrong. As long as horses can stand up and bear riders, so long they do duty. Contemplating from the middle of the ring the results of his prowess, the bull repeated the pleasing performance, when the picador again mounted.

There are many variations; but the theme never varies, and, before the act closed, six horses lay stark and stiff. Spaniards are intensely critical in the matter of bull-fights. When they think they are being cheated out of sport, they do not hesitate to cry for more horses, and in trepidation the managers rush into the street to buy the first cheap hack that offers. Twenty-five dollars apiece is the price generally paid. Six dead horses in one act satisfy the most exacting. Now came the mules. Harnessed three abreast, with nodding flags and tassels, they were driven in to fast music, and performed scavenger duty by dragging off their dead relations in a *tempo furioso*. The entrails were raked up, and Act Second began.

Showing no signs of fatigue, Christopher Columbus's bull made work for the *capeadores* (the men who shake their cloaks about promiscuously), and fiercely eyed the *banderilleros* (from *bande-*

rilla, little banner), who, in the gorgeous livery of Figaro, entered the ring, bearing barbs which must be lodged artistically in the bull's neck. Now set in the contest between brute instinct and human skill. Not to poise the barbs in the right place is to excite multitudinous indignation; therefore the banderillero is ever on the alert, coquetting with the bull until the moment for throwing arrives. If the barbs are aimed finely, and go in straight, the banderillero becomes a hero. He bows, he receives a shower of cigars, men throw him their hats, which he returns with masterly flings, and the owners are made happy. Picture, if you can, the inexpressible joy of seeing six of these murderous barbs — six or eight being the number allowed — standing erect in the bull's neck. Tortured, frenzied, the poor beast still showed pluck. Had he not, there would have been loud cries of "Fuego, fuego," and barbs with fireworks would have been fastened upon his back to give him additional vivacity. With the throwing of the third pair of barbs Act Second ended.

Act Third disclosed the *espada* (swordsman), vulgarly called *matador* (slayer), humoring, coaxing, teasing the bull by dexterously handling the cloak, under which was the weapon destined to do the final butchering. The espada, Lagartijo (Little Lizard), was received with great favor, and certainly he knew every trick of his noble trade. That bull would not give up, but Lagartijo proved equal to the occasion. He magnetized the bull, which for a second was thrown off his guard. In that second, Lagartijo planted the sword between the bull's horns and the splendid animal dropped dead. Great was the cheering, many were the hats thrown, more were the cigars. An attendant picked them up, and Lagartijo, with his blue velvet costume embroidered in silver, with his white silk stock-

ings, and with his black hair done up in a pig-
tail, felt that his supreme ambition had been
realized.

The Espada's last Thrust.

Living mules bore off the dead bull, and there
followed an intermission for discussion, cigarettes,
and water. Two men below me went into a
bull-like passion over the recent sport. They
howled, screamed, shook their fists; one gave
the other the lie direct; the other seized his
opponent by the throat, and put the wretch's

head between his knees. In a minute more there would have been a dead brute of another species, had not a woman interposed. Fourteen thousand people talked at once. The police interfered; the combatants were marched off, glaring fiendishly at each other; the woman followed, and the excitement subsided. Such are the soothing effects of bull-fights.

A flourish of abominable music, and Bull No. 2 rushed into the ring. He was young and black, totally unlike his brother. It is comparatively easy to judge of bulls on inspection; but to be *au fait* in bull-fighters demands far more experience. Every bull-fight requires different tactics, and I understand a certain amount of interest being excited in humane minds unaccustomed to the sport, after the slaughtering of the horses has been gone through. Mexico, more merciful than Spain, does away with horses altogether. With the establishment of a real republic the old country may adopt the reforms of the new.

This young bull did not know what to make of the scene. He had no disposition to hurt anybody, consequently his audience informed him that he disgraced Christopher Columbus, that he was no better than he should be, that he was a beast. Spurred on by these taunts, he proceeded to gore the nearest horse and unseat his rider, who, not showing a disposition to mount again, listened to the gratifying chorus of "Coward!" It is excessively brave for men secure from danger to bully those who run a certain amount of risk. The picador grew very red in the face, gesticulated profusely, and finally remounted the ripped-up horse. Bull No. 2, however, seemed unwilling to fight. He tossed his head and pawed the ground. He believed in peace. He refused to shed the blood for which thousands thirsted, and when the first banderillero launched his barbs his bullship jumped over the barrier, much to the scattering of venturesome spectators. There was no escape, and back he went to be butchered. Butchered he was, for the espada ran the sword in bunglingly, the bull shook it out, and the work had to be done over again. I was spared the extra barbarity of the *media luna*, which consists in cutting the tendons of the bull's hind legs with a long-handled instrument shaped like a half-moon, so that the poor creature may fall and be despatched with a knife. This is resorted to when the espada utterly fails.

Thus ended the second bull. The third was as game as the first, the fourth as young and *naïve* as the second, the fifth not unlike the first and third. By this time the spectacle grew intolerable. To see fair young women, boys, girls, white-headed men enthusiastic over a one-sided sport, in which all the animals but man are sure of death, excites a mingled feeling of indignation and disgust. The Rhode-Islander stood with his face to the wall. He kicked the back of the box, I rapped the front. This was our only outlet for pent-up feelings. "The Spaniards are brutes," exclaimed the Rhode-Islander. "They are not fit for a republic," said I. Then I bethought me that this was hardly just. It is possible to be kind-hearted and yet enjoy a bull-fight. Theophile Gautier — Heaven rest his brilliant soul! — once declared that a bull-fight was one of the finest spectacles imaginable to man, and that when civilization destroyed bull-fights, it would be so much the worse for civilization. And Gautier was an artist. The New-Yorker who sat beside me had the tenderest of hearts, but, from much experience, took an interest in the duel between man and bull. What we drink in with mother's milk we accept without criticism. Children that play Toro with a basket bull are likely to view the real game unmoved by pity. Horrible as the sport may be, it is not the ghastly thing in which Rome once took pleasure. What Italian would relish a bull-fight? As Rome has grown out of brutality, so may Spain. The republican leaders dislike bull-fights, but it would cost them their heads to suggest abolition. Sooner will Spain voluntarily free her slaves, and grant Cuban independence, than connive at the suppression of her "peculiar institution." She will not forswear it until she has learned to prize fair play beyond fair words.

Leaving the sickening scene, we drove in the miniature Hyde Park, and saw as much of fashion as had returned to town. It was Paris over again. The women wore French clothes, and the men were the same pale, *blasé* creatures I had left in the Bois de Boulogne. Society that goes about on wheels is identical all the world over. I beheld neither the typical Spanish man nor woman. Never have I seen any traditional type of nationality as strongly marked on its own soil as it is found in America. There are more Greek heads in the United States than in Greece. The purest classical profile known to me is that of a New England woman. Mixture of races seems to produce the characteristic beauties of all.

Near the Plaza de Toros is the Cock-Pit. Performances at the latter place begin at noon, so that Madrid can take its cock-fighting *en route* to its bulls. What economy in high-bred pleasure! And why should it be fashionable for women to witness the disembowelling of blinded horses and not the fury of equally matched cocks? There is so much more manliness in the latter as to render it eminently respectable when compared with the former. Half-way between cocks and bulls is the palace of Marshal Serrano, who appears to occupy a similar position between Republicanism and Carlism. He is a shrewd man. Does this signify that half-way between Castelar and Don Carlos lie the probabilities of Spanish government?

On returning from the drive I received an invitation to dine. What a comfortable sensation it was to sit down before a real table at the Café Forno — Madrid's Delmonico's — and eat a tolerable French dinner! I had breakfasted at the hotel, but delusively. The steak had tenderness without taste; the *purée* of potatoes might as well have been paper in a pulpy state of mash. Owing to the worn-out condition of the soil, neither Spanish meats nor vegetables possess any flavor; among fruits, watermelons and grapes alone are grateful to the taste. Flavor is confined to butter and onions. Of the latter, a very little goes a great way; of the former, the very least goes no way at all with one not to the butter born. It is simply impossible, and well deserves the name of " hog's lard " ! I do not refer to olives, because they are exceptionally fine and

prove the rule. There is no country in Europe
with so horrible a *cuisine* as Spain. This is the
dominant reason why self-respecting travellers
carefully avoid it. Not all the traditional beauties of Andalusia can compensate for prolonged
insult to a liberally educated stomach. Do not
languishing black eyes pale in the presence of
pork and garlic?

After dinner came the ballet, and did I not
see Emerson's Brahma, "the Doubter and the
doubt," burnt alive in the arms of a young lady
in short skirts with whom he was enamored?
There is nothing like a ballet for unmitigated
historical veracity. After the ballet was there
not the going home, catching glimpses of cafés
saturated with black coats, cigarettes, and *eau
sucré*? I retired to the soothing accompaniment
of café buzzing, feeling satisfied that my first
day in Madrid could not have been fuller had
it been packed as piles are driven.

PART V.

Emilio Castelar.

6 *

V.

The Gallery of Paintings at Madrid. — A Visit to Emilio Castelar. — Talks with Bourgeois, Office-Holders, and the Blinker, on the Prospects of Republicanism.

MADRID is most satisfactory to travellers in a hurry who are morbid on the subject of embracing opportunities. There are no opportunities to embrace. It is an inexpressible comfort to know that you cannot improve your mind. Churches do not lie in wait for you, nor do ruins upbraid you for not sketching them on the spot. After visiting the fine armory, beholding the Cid's sword and the armor worn by Charles V. and by Christopher Columbus, — both men of medium size, — there is nothing to see but the picture-gallery; and the gallery, as the world knows, is everything to see. It is a wilderness of genius, thrown together with Spanish contempt for order and chronology, absolutely stupefying in its. first effect, gradually fascinating, until appreciative souls stand spellbound before its masterpieces. Far better, however, is the arrangement of the gallery than in 1828, when David Wilkie, the Scotch painter, was obliged to appeal to his own government before being able to gain access to the Flemish paintings that had lured him to Spain.

Nothing is easier than fine writing about painting and sculpture. I'll none of it. Critics, not *littérateurs*, are needed for this work. When Hawthorne, in "The Marble Faun," undertook to play the connoisseur, and praise his artist friends, he displayed ignorance and amiable weakness unworthy of his literary genius. Fancy makes fiction and mars criticism. But it is no fiction to express enthusiasm for the portraiture of Velasquez. Painting more honest, more manly, cannot be conceived. I'd rather have one Velasquez than a dozen Murillos, for there is a virility, a scorn for nonsense and sentimentality, a respect for reality, however unlovely, that brace the soul to renew its fight for truth. Were history written as Velasquez painted it, we should have facts, not prejudice. He has insured immortality to his royal patrons. Their worst deeds will be forgotten before their faces. Nevertheless, while reverencing Valasquez, I pity him. The Spanish Court condemned him for life to the painting of ugly men and women. There is not a sympathetic face among all the Bourbons. What this artist, with his love for beauty, must have endured, no one but himself can tell, and I fancy that he painted his wonderful portrait of Bohemian Æsop as a protest against royal ruffs and imbecility.

Cold chills ran down my back at sight of narrow-headed boys and sleek young women copying Murillos, intended, probably, for American drawing-rooms. Why men and women possessed of ordinary sense pay gold for painted blasphemies of old masters, when for very little money they can purchase excellent photographs, defies comprehension.

On returning to the hotel after my first visit to the gallery, I met the kindest of men with the most amiable of letters. The man was our Secretary of Legation, a cultivated American, who is manna in the wilderness to travellers hungering for companionship tempered with valuable information. He is a gentleman and a guidebook complete in one person, and an honor to our diplomatic service. Would there were more like him! From whom came the letter he held up for me to read? The superscription was addressed to "Señor Adee, Secretario de la Legacion de los Estados Unidos," and at the foot of the envelope I beheld "Emilio Castelar," distinct and upright, with a slight flourish beneath. The President of the Spanish Republic is a boon to autograph-maniacs. He signs in full both envelope and letter. Peeping inside, I saw a plain violet monogram of E. C. in the left-hand corner, and read how, on the following day at noon, the President would be disengaged; how he would be happy to receive his dear friend the Secretary's compatriot in *her* house, and how, had he known her residence, he would have called. Here at least was a man who, having power thrust upon him, assumed no official dignity, content to stand or fall by personal worth. Details denote character. So far I liked Emilio Castelar.

Precisely at noon on the following day a cab left me before the President's door. There was a shop on the ground-floor, and one soldier only, in fatigue dress, defended the general entrance.

I mounted three flights of stairs before arriving at Castelar's apartment. He is a bachelor, living with a sister older than himself; a sister who tells wonderful stories of her brother's memory, — how, as a boy, he could repeat verbatim the contents of a newspaper after one perusal, and how he never forgets anything he reads. Castelar must be particular in his choice of books, for what a terrible trial it would be to most of us to remember all we read! On ringing the bell, a man without livery appeared. Señor Castelar would be disengaged shortly. Nothing could be plainer than the two small rooms into which I was ushered. Engravings of the Spanish masters hung upon the walls. Besides these, a bronze statuette of Don Quixote, another of Mirabeau, a few books, and an enormous bouquet, as uncouth as Europe could make it (and Europe excels in hideous floral arrangements), were the sole ornaments. Had I not known of Castelar's sister,

I should have said the rooms lacked the touch
of a woman's hand; but few Continental apartments look like homes. Cosiness is an Anglo-
Saxon specialty. Latin drawing-rooms resemble
our hotel parlors in small, and as Spanish families move whenever there is a death among
them, they exist without roots. Though Americans move oftener than the English, our homes
are the prettiest, most comfortable and convenient in the world. We have no palaces, no
state apartments; but who that has breathed
the cold atmosphere of colossal grandeur wishes
to live in it?

All this I thought while waiting for Castelar,
becoming more and more nervous about seeing
him; for what right had I to take up his valuable time, — I who had come to Spain solely to
look at him, hear him talk if he would, and draw
my own conclusions for my own satisfaction?
I had not been sent on a mission by a great

moral organ; I was not clothed in the garb of an interviewer. Impulse alone had impelled me, and how could I draw Castelar out in half an hour? Though I might long to put leading questions and jump into the middle of things, I could not. *Noblesse oblige.* I had begun to snub impulse, and wish myself on the other side of the Pyrenees, when Castelar entered, shaking hands so cordially as to render my rôle less difficult than I had feared. He was a man of thirty-six, about five feet six inches tall, inclined to corpulency, squarely built and short-necked. He had an olive complexion, great, black, sympathetic eyes, denoting a near-sightedness that the glasses hanging from his neck proved; a round face, shorn of all but a heavy black mustache, concealing the mouth too much to please a physiognomist; a round, good-natured chin; a noble, dome-shaped head, somewhat suggestive of Shakespeare's, benevolent to others, yet ungenerous to itself in the matter of hair. This was Emilio Castelar; he too introverted to remark the ink-stain upon his shirt or the general carelessness of his dress. Enemies make capital out of this personal negligence. It shows how clean Castelar must be

Emilio Castelar.

inside when opponents are obliged to attack his clothes. A clever Spaniard, immaculate in attire, once devoted a whole hour to the task of demonstrating Castelar's unfitness to govern because of his slovenliness. I admired the handsome Spaniard, but failed to be convinced. Cleanliness is next to godliness; but if, in revolutionary times, we cannot have both, let us take godliness and be grateful.

What first rises to the surface in Castelar is exceeding amiability. Thoroughly unassuming, not anxious to speak of himself, he turned the conversation upon America, expressing great interest in our government, wanting to know about the condition of the South, and regretting that he did not speak English. He could read it, and was very fond of Emerson, but to talk it was beyond his power. Castelar speaks French, but not purely. The Cortes had closed its doors three days before, so I could not hear him at his best. Americans have assured me that Castelar excited them to the highest pitch, although speaking a language unknown to them. His pantomime and fervor inspired an enthusiasm for they could not tell what! This is indeed oratory.

"Ah, I love the tribune, — I love speaking!" exclaimed Castelar, in the tone of one not quite at home in his new position.

"Then you are thrust into power! You accept the Presidency because there is no one else?"

"Precisely."

It seemed to me Castelar uttered the absolute truth. It seemed to me he realized what Nature had intended him for, — authorship and oratory. It seemed to me his highest ambition was to help establish republicanism in his own country. Rather than have the experiment fail, he had taken command. I recognized the lovable man, the author and orator, but I could not see the born statesman. His jaw lacked such force as a physiognomist would declare necessary to drag Spain out of mire and bankruptcy. I am sure his spinal column is short. Long spines denote executive ability. A leader

should have profound knowledge of men. I
could not feel Castelar to be in any sense a
man of the world. "I am always inclined to
believe more good than evil of human nature,"
he writes in "Old Rome and New Italy," and I
thought that too much faith in the promises of
others, an impossibility to conceive treachery,
would sooner or later cause his downfall. Unlike his people, he impressed me not only as
above suspicion, but so constituted as to be
incapable of it. Seeing everything *couleur de
rôse* is charming in society, but not safe in gov-
erning, where the worst should be anticipated.
All the while I thought, "What a good fellow
you are, and what a lamb you will be among
those Spanish foxes quietly plotting against you!
May Providence interpose and save you from
your own unsuspecting self!"

Much that Castelar said was confidential.
What I repeat, therefore, is of comparatively

little interest. At the time (September 23) the
Spanish army of the North did not equal the
Carlists in numbers. On the following week
there would be reinforcements. Then Castelar
hoped for favorable results. Months have since
gone by, and Don Carlos still holds his own. The
Intransigente were almost crushed out. They
are not dead yet. With three wars going on
at once, — Cuban, Carlist, and Intransigente, —
I might judge whether he, Castelar, had not
enough to do. Mark you, Castelar acknowl-
edged there was a war in Cuba, although the
Spanish government does not. He worked from
eight in the morning until midnight, taking very
little exercise. This is bad policy for a bilious
temperament subject to fearful headaches. Men
with self-asserting livers are not the best to
handle intricate reins. Vertigo may come at
any moment, and then where are the passengers ? For the sake of the republic Castelar
is impairing his health.

"When would slavery be abolished?"

"Soon."

"And what means soon?"

"When the Cortes meets."

The Cortes has met, and deposed not slavery, but Castelar. Consistency is not a jewel to be found in Spain.

"But how is it, Señor Castelar," I asked, "that you, who throughout your public career have asserted the right to self-government, should persist in holding Cuba, in spite of having buried 80,000 soldiers and a vast amount of treasure?"

"Ah, I see that you do not sympathize with Spain in this matter."

"Most decidedly not. I believe in Cuba Libre."

Castelar looked at me. He would not argue because he could not. No man cares to eat his own words. No diet is more indigestible.

"My two great ideas, whose worship I shall

never renounce, are liberty and country," wrote Castelar in "Old Rome and New Italy." Said he to me, quietly: "I am first a Spaniard, and then a Republican." In days of power country comes first; liberty must look out for itself. Very differently did Castelar talk to Charles Bradlaugh; but times had changed. In the spring Castelar was out of office; in the autumn he was dictator. I know in what a difficult position he was placed; I know that justice to Cuba meant signing his own political death-warrant; but for all that Castelar stultified himself. I saw that he would sacrifice one republic to found another; that he could not resist the temptation of resorting to Jesuitical dogma, — the end justified the means. And I saw that Cuba had no more to gain from Spain, so-called republican, than from Spain monarchical.

You may paint, you may flatter, "free" Spain as you will,
But the scent of the bloodhound will hang round it still.

7   J

In betraying the dream of his youth, Castelar made a fearful mistake, which he may rue in exile. The Spanish republic is not worth founding if it can only exist at the expense of colonial despotism. Spain cannot be a republic as long as she clutches Cuba by the throat, nor will she be a republic in name any longer than suits the convenience of monarchical factions. Better far for Castelar's fame had his watchword been that of the past, — "Liberty and Country." True to it, he would be loved by all republicans. Now he is doubted by many, and hated by Cuba. Is anything in the world worth the renunciation of sworn principles?

Had Señor Castelar faith in the permanency of the republic? Yes. Spain was republican; much more so than France. The bourgeoisie and people were republican, and with the reorganization of the army, there would be changes for the better.

I had remained longer than ceremony permitted. It behooved me to go, and I rose to say farewell, when Castelar changed it to *au revoir*, adding that he would call upon me. He named the hour and day, and I took my leave, feeling that I had known Castelar almost as long as I had liked him. But — I felt more uncertain about the republic than before making a delightful acquaintance.

On leaving the house I was importuned by beggars. I asked them what their politics were. They replied with a grin that they had none. What they wanted was enough to eat and drink. Why should they care for anything else? "St. Christopher take everybody that keeps strangers away and makes money scarce!" Paying the beggars for their valuable remarks, I sauntered into a shop for the purpose of chatting with one of the bourgeoisie. There were photographs for sale, and the young man behind the counter ad-

dressed me in English, saying that, although he
had lived in Spain all his life, his mother was
Scotch and his father French. The civil war
had made foreigners so rare that the clerk
seemed to look upon me as a blessing in disguise, and we immediately launched into conversation. There is nothing like photography
to let loose the flow of talk. What were the
specialties of Madrid? Why, there were photographs of the Spanish masters, but those might
be bought in Paris. What thrived only on
home soil were bull-fights and bull-fighters. Out
came numerous bull-fighters in every possible
attitude, all of whom I bought and studied.
They are not a bad-looking lot. Their figures
are lithe, their heads are not brutally built,
there is nothing of the prize-fighter about their
necks. Mouths alone tell the story of their
lives. Without exception they are sensual in
the worst acceptation, hard, and often cruel. I

thought of the fine duchesses, who, on several
occasions, had invited noted *espadas* to dinner,
— duchesses who could not have been induced
to extend similar courtesies to distinguished
lyric or dramatic artists ; and I realized how
much American society has to learn from its
mother. We never give dinner-parties to heroes
of the ring who make jelly of one another in
far more manly style than the Spanish heroes
draw blood. We are still young ; we may come
to it.

There were photographs of the bulls killed
at the previous fight. Fine creatures, were they
not ? I bought them as a tender souvenir.
Would I look at the fans illustrating the national sport ? Of course. I bought one. Would
I purchase the book of colored prints giving a
most accurate idea of a bull-fight from beginning to end ? Certainly. No lady's library
could be complete without it. There were pica-

dors sticking lances into bulls, bulls tossing dogs, and horses galloping about in a state of hari-kari. What more entertaining to an educated mind?

"Now," said I, having had enough of blood and bulls, "I want photographs of your public men."

That irreverent clerk began to laugh. "Madam," he exclaimed, "which? If you buy them all, you will purchase the greater part of our stock. We've a lot of public men in Spain. We've the Carlists, the Bourbons, the Amade-ists, the Alphonsists, the Republicans, the In-transigentes, the Montpensierists, and anything else you please. You see everybody is poor here, and everybody wants to live off the gov-ernment without doing any work. So men stay in office until they rob the treasury as much as they dare, and then retire on a personal mis-understanding."

I began with the beginning, Her Most Catholic Majesty Isabella Segunda. In her ordinary costume she needs but a dozen children and a wash-tub to be a counterfeit presentment of the typical Biddy. In court dress Her Majesty resembles a hideous, over-stuffed pincushion shaped like an ungainly bell. "She's a good riddance," said the clerk. "Spaniards can stand a great deal. They enjoy gossip, and there never was so much scandal talked as in Madrid; but the Queen went too far, and they were all glad when she departed. Here's the photograph of Marshal Serrano, the man who conspired against her. Isn't it Spanish for the Queen to be driven out of her palace by an old lover?" Yes, it is very Spanish and very like Serrano, for I remember what the Duchess of Victoria said to Washington Irving when, on the deposition of her husband from the Vice-Regency, Serrano offered her an escort out of Spain : "Serrano professed

to be my husband's friend; he rose by his friend-
ship and favors, and he proved faithless to him.
I will accept nothing at his hands, and beg his
name may not again be mentioned to me."

"The next thing Serrano will do, if he is not
up to it already," continued the loquacious clerk,
"will be to plot for the return of Don Alphonso
and make himself Regent. This is the game
most likely to succeed. His wife, a most ambi-
tious woman, — that photograph with the long
nose and insincere mouth is she, — will do all in
her power to overthrow the republic. The aris-
tocracy has the money, wants a court, and will
have one. The Spaniards love show. One great
fault they found with Amadeo was his simplicity
in living. They did n't like his conducting himself after the manner of ordinary people. I 've
seen him walk past here unaccompanied, followed
by boys whose jeering forced him to take refuge
in a shop. 'At least our Queen, with all her

infidelities, know how to preserve her dignity in public,' I have heard Spaniards exclaim. They want state carriages and pomp. You ought to see a religious procession in this town. There is no such private and public display in any other part of Europe. Amadeo was a perfect gentleman, yet he never succeeded in making himself popular. He and his wife did not agree about the church. He hated priests, and always enjoyed their discomfiture. She was very pious; consequently between them they contrived to displease everybody, for the clerical party hated the King, and the liberal party mistrusted his wife. Here is a photograph of Amadeo and his suite, paying their last respects to the dead body of Prim. There was an outrage for you. A woman did that. Now, I like the Spaniards exceedingly in many ways, but they think nothing of murder. A little money is all one needs to get rid of an uncomfortable enemy."

7 *

I recalled the execution of 7,000 Cubans in five years, and thought that perhaps the garrulous clerk was not entirely wrong.

"And they think nothing of stealing. Many a cigar that I have laid down for a moment has been appropriated by some one of our workmen. They are not brought up with our ideas. Instead of morals, they have superstitions. But they are frequently kind and obliging. They have good qualities, and any one living among them must acknowledge the fact."

Next we passed to the Carlists. There is a jauntiness about the military men suggestive of the theatre, and Don Carlos himself makes an attractive picture. Very dark, with regular features and full black beard, he seems a gentleman, but the weakness of his mouth betrays absence of intellect. After seeing his photograph I was ready to regard him as a willing tool in the hands of others, — his wife, perhaps. Santa

Cruz, the ex-Queen's ex-confessor, arrayed in the nondescript garb of a Carlist scout, looked the incarnation of a cut-throat. A more brutal physiognomy I never saw.

Don Carlos.

Lastly we came to the Republicans, beginning with Castelar. For the first time I beheld thoughtful faces. None of them, however, impressed me as men of action or of great business capacity. I saw why Castelar had been placed at their head, and I pitied the republic.

"Have you or your friends faith in the existence of the present government?"

"Government? There is none. Everybody is waiting for something to happen. Castelar is a fine man and a great orator, but you can't make a coat when you have no cloth. The Spaniards are too ignorant to sustain a man like Castelar for any length of time. The very poorest people sympathize with the Intransigentes; but I don't meet any persons who are willing to fight for Castelar's republic. He is accepted *faute de mieux*. Spain is not America, you know."

Armed with my package of photographs, I next strolled into a public building, for no other purpose than to chat with the custodian, who was the picture of benevolence.

"Are you a republican?" I asked.

The amiable old man smiled and shook his head. No, indeed. He liked no such ideas. He was a Carlist. He would do nothing against the government : he was too old to fight, and his family required his help. If Don Carlos came, however, he would rejoice.

Where should I find a Castelar republican ? I thought I discovered him in the guise of another government doorkeeper, a young man with fiery eyes; but he too proved delusive.

"Yes," he said, "I 'm a republican, but not such as those who are experimenting now, although I admire Señor Castelar. The Intransigentes offered to make me a captain if I would join them, but there are too many rascals among them. They want to burn everything, and I don't."

Endeavoring to ascertain the young fellow's principles, I found them excessively vague; but two things he would not do, — he would acknowledge allegiance to neither Castelar nor Cartagena. They might settle their own quarrels. He would criticise and bide his time. This he knew : he hated those black flies, the priests. They had made the Queen what she was.

Going back to the hotel, I rang for the Blinker, whose sole instructions had been to buy three pounds of grapes a day and spend the rest of the time in finding out what shopkeepers and such people as he came in contact with thought of republicanism. The Blinker was himself as democratic as a flunky could be; so I knew, if he lied at all, he would lie on the right side.

" Well, what do Spaniards say to you about the government ? "

" Madam, I have known the Spaniards twenty-six years — "

" Yes, I am aware of that fact. Never mind what happened twenty-six years ago. Tell me what happens now."

" Pardon, madam. In twenty-six years I have never known the Spaniards as queer as they are now. They do nothing but abuse everybody. They are discontented, madam, and don't seem to know what they want. They call Señor Castelar a '*charmant garçon*,' who means well; but they insist that Spain is not republican, and they expect a change in a few months. They would rather have Castelar than Don Carlos; but if Don Alphonso were of age, they would clamor for him. It looks as though he would come back, instead of his mother. The Alphonsists appear wise, madam. They are respectable people, and the shopkeepers want a court. Nobody spends money now. Señor Castelar does not even keep a carriage."

"Do you mean to say that you meet no real republicans?"

"Parfaitement, madame."

Was my search to be as hopeless as that of Diogenes?

PART VI.

The Escorial and Toledo.

K

VI.

A Child of the Escorial. — Spain's Eighth Wonder of the World.
— The Tagus. — Toledo's Streets and only Hotel. Mental Dyspepsia. — Frozen Music. — The Toledan Cathedral and Alcazar.
— A Carlist.

I MIGHT have had two comfortable days at Madrid for the study of Velasquez and Murillo, had not public opinion been too much for me. When Castelar asked whether I were going to Andalusia, where he was born, and I answered, "No," he said I would see nothing of Spain. I knew it; but, not having visited Spain to become acquainted with the country, I bore up under the President's astonished gaze. Seville was far away, comparatively, and I could defy criticism concerning it; but

when the Escorial and Toledo were mentioned,
my courage oozed out at the pores. Both were
too near Madrid to be ignored, and I "did"
them on successive days. First came the Escorial, — built by Herrera, "architect of *ennui*," —
the eighth wonder of the world according to
Spanish criticism; the monstrous conception of
that tyrant, monk, and hypochondriac, Philip
II., according to my own. I am not Murray.
I don't propose to furnish information that will
be of the slightest use to the most inexperienced
traveller. All I shall relate is what stuck to
me like burrs after the guide had poured the
entire Escorial into my aching ears. And he
was an excellent guide, mark you. He had a
conscience. His father had been a guide before
him. He was, as it were, a child of the Escorial, and felt that the eyes of the Bourbons
were upon him. He made shoes in the dull
season, but all seasons were dull nowadays, he

said, and it was very hard to provide for his family. He did n't know how the war would end, for his part. He was quite tired of commotion. He would like an intelligent government that educated the people. Whatever happened, he should submit. That which most concerned him was the welfare of his wife and children.

I did my utmost to excite the guide, but I might as well have attempted to make the Escorial dance. There was a repose about him that would have done credit to the remains of Philip II. Perpetual contact with dead kings seemed to have wrought a spell upon him. On his brow I read "All is vanity." His gait illustrated the dignity of Spain. In his conversation there was such submission to fate as is sometimes visible in very much married men and women. Artemus Ward's best joke could not have undermined his gravity.

"Tell me," I said, "are all the inhabitants of this place as serious as you?"

"There are but a few hundred, Señora. We are all more or less connected with the Escorial. Our lives are quiet. We are poor. What is there to laugh at? We behave ourselves. The jail is always empty. In other parts of Spain men stab one another. Here the knife is unknown. The only instance of crime I remember is recent. Two small and valuable paintings were stolen, and, as their custodian could not account for their disappearance, he has been imprisoned, but not here. He was sent to Madrid. When people want bread, Señora, they cannot think of much else."

Was it not my turn to be serious?

Five long hours I wandered over the great, yellow, barren, gloomy building, resting only on the finely carved bench in the church choir, where Philip II. used to sit.

"He sat here," said the guide, "because a secret door communicates with it. He could

come and go without being observed, and so
he kept the monks on the alert, I assure you.
They treated themselves tenderly, nevertheless.
The seats, you perceive, turn down. This is in
order to afford standing-room when their occu-
pants rise; but those monks did not like being
on their feet. You remark the shelves arranged
above the seats? On them the monks sat while
appearing to stand up. Ah, ah! this is very
shrewd, very ingenious." And the guide almost
smiled. It was such an attempt at a smile as
becomes funerals.

The guide was a good Catholic, but he entertained very little regard for priests. In this,
however, he is not peculiar. "Our religion is
one thing, our clergy quite another," assert all
the Latin Catholics I know. "We don't wish
to become Protestants. All we desire is that
our church shall mind its legitimate business,
and not interfere with temporal affairs."

A granite gridiron, covering a regular parallelogram of 200 metres, containing 1010 outside windows, consuming twenty-one years in construction, costing unknown millions of francs, arising in the midst of an arid, mountainous wilderness — for what? To celebrate the miserable pride and bigotry of a bad king. Thank Heaven, even Spain can never repeat the enormous, hideous burlesque of the Escorial. Apart from harboring a few paintings and a library of rare books, art gains nothing by it; and the time is not far distant when Madrid will claim both books and canvas. On the ground-floor of one wing can still be seen half a dozen old masters, one of which, a Rubens, so delighted the present Emperor of Brazil that he offered to build a fine hospital in exchange for it; but the government did not dare to entertain the proposition. In the dark corner of an obscure room I was shown an unframed portrait of

Isabella Segunda. "We put her here, Señora, to have her out of harm's way; otherwise she would be cut to pieces." In a neighboring gallery stood a clever wooden statue of St. Michael overcoming the Devil. "That has a history," said the guide. "It is the work of a very talented female sculptor. St. Michael's face is her own. Handsome, was she not? Satan's face is her husband's. Her lover was the king whose portrait hangs opposite, and the eyes of which are fixed upon St. Michael. If you write, Señora, behold good material!"

Of course I visited the dark den once inhabited by Philip II. Of course I sat on the two chairs dedicated to his gout, — Summer and Winter. Both were as hard as the monarch's heart; and then, by the aid of a tallow candle, I descended to the octagonal crypt where repose the mortal remains of twenty-six Spanish kings and queens. Cold, cold, almost as cold as the dead, I read the

8

names of Charles V., Philip II., and Philip IV. I saw five empty shelves, and I predicted that not more than one would ever be occupied. "You'll have little more royalty to stow away," I said to the guide.

The last resting-place of royalty.

"I do not say you are wrong, Señora, but who can tell? You've no idea what a people we are! Anything may happen to-morrow."

"Mañana." There it was again.

The Royal Gridiron has many corners. I do believe I went into every one of them. Church and palace were " done " religiously, and when, dragging one slow leg after the other, I finally reached the station, in default of chairs I dropped into a wheelbarrow and asked to be let alone.

" It is well, Señora," remarked the guide; " you have walked twenty miles."

" It is not the walking, Mr. Guide, it is the miles I have stood up. How many are they?"

Strangely enough the guide could not tell me. The Blinker attempted to make a remark, but, as usual, threw no light upon the subject; and, when the Madrid train arrived, only an hour late, I crawled into a compartment, feeling as though I had supported the dome of the Escorial ever since its existence.

" Long life to you, Señora. I hope I have given you satisfaction," exclaimed the guide. Satisfaction ! He had given me such an amount

that I ached from head to foot. I knew so
much as to hope never to know anything again.
Fortunately "cramming" escapes into thin air,
otherwise sight-seers would blow themselves up
in a manner calculated to terrify high-pressure
steamboats.

Being quite alive the next morning, the Blinker
and I started at six o'clock for Toledo. The
amount of effort required to leave my bed, and,
as usual, go without breakfast, drew so largely
on my moral courage that I felt another such
call would kill me. In flying to evils that you
know not of there is the bliss of ignorance, but
in deliberately embracing slow torture there is
not even the satisfaction of novelty. Between
travelling on a snail's back and a Spanish railroad there is little choice, saving in matter of
accommodation. The road to Toledo is no better
than that of the North, while the scenery is infinitely worse. Flat and uncultivated, the coun-

try seemed branded with a curse, and not until we arrived at Aranjuez, half-way between Madrid and Toledo, did life begin to assert itself. Having no curiosity to inspect the "Spanish Fontainebleau," where once stood a temple of Jupiter, — Ara Jovis, hence Aranjuez, — I accepted it on faith, contenting myself with glimpses of that "mighty river," the Tagus, 375 miles long, yet so inhospitable as to receive few towns upon its banks and to welcome no commerce upon its waters. No sensation could be extracted from it. Mud is mud, though called the Tagus, and if I must gaze upon rivers of it, give me my own, my native Mississippi.

At noon I saw a city set on a hill. We stopped. It was Toledo. Leaving the cars at a ragged station and running the gantlet of beggars, — there were twenty beggars to three passengers, giving us six beggars and two thirds of a beggar apiece, — we took refuge in a remarkable vehicle, courteously called an omnibus, the only public conveyance known to Toledo. Passenger No. 3 hobnobbed with the Blinker, and exhibited a curiosity regarding our movements that would have brought a blush to even a Yankee cheek. The driver, a man of immense stature, scowled at us for not being more numerous, and, with a round oath and much snapping of his long whip, started his four mules up the hill. Why Spanish mules should wear bells, and why they should require so much beating, I don't know, but they certainly get a deal of both. Every saint in the calendar was called upon by the driver to witness the ingratitude, the obstinacy, the total depravity, of those animated mules, that I thought were exerting themselves to pieces. Through clouds of dust we whirled over the bridge of Alcantara, thrown across the deep-set, winding Tagus, up a second steep hill, in and out of the narrowest, queerest, quaintest, most impossible streets, under an archway, and then we found ourselves at the Fonda de Lino, the only hotel the guide-books dare to mention.

"First I want something to eat, and then I want the guide Cabezas," said I to the proprietor, on descending from the noble omnibus.

"You can't have Cabezas," replied the ever-important Blinker, "because he is dead."

"How do you know?"

"Because he was buried shortly after my last visit to Toledo."

"Who says I'm dead? I'm nothing of the sort. I'm as alive as he, Señora." And up hobbled a withered old man, who was no other than Cabezas himself.

It is not pleasant to be told you are dead and buried before you have stopped breathing. Cabezas looked cross, but the Blinker received him with a pitying smile, as if to say, "I accept your apology for being alive, but don't do it again, my old fellow. You ought to be dead, you know. Be sure you are so before I return."

Though alive and hobbling, Cabezas, who knows every nail and stone of Toledo, could not accompany me in my tour of the tortuous old town, "because you see, Señora, there are two guides and very little to do. You are the first foreigner we have had for a month. We divide the work. I went last, so the other guide, who is good, must go with you."

Colonel John Hay, in his charming "Castilian Days," the atmosphere of which is as clear and bright as Castile itself, advises travellers to ignore guides at Toledo; nevertheless, if Colonel Hay had but a few hours to devote to many centuries, I think he would hire the fastest possible engine to rush through them. Who can saunter with one eye on a watch and the other on a railroad?

If the Fonda de Lino be a specimen of Toledan

housekeeping, I am not surprised that the number of inhabitants has been reduced from 200,000 to 17,000. The marvel is that anybody can be prevailed upon to remain over night, or, remaining, does not die before morning. The longer I live the more amazed I become at the quantities of people in existence. Ushered into the eating-room, I sat before a table at which several Spaniards were devouring knives and pork. Not being able to digest either, I ordered beefsteak and tea, whereupon the Spaniards nudged one another and said, "English!" When the steak came I shuddered. It was very thin, very stringy, very young, had been fried, and was flavored with vinegar. The bread was sour, and the tea! well, it was that pink kind of tea, found only in Italy and Spain, which tastes like some unknown medicine and excites a mild form of nausea as it goes down. Pounds would not make it strong enough to come up again.

Thus fortified, I began my pilgrimage. Guide-books state that it requires a year to become acquainted with Toledo. More exacting still, M. Villa Amil declares that after studying its treasures nine months you know nothing about them. This is encouraging to a traveller on the wing, particularly after being presented with a monograph entitled *Toledo en la mano,* in two volumes of 1550 pages. After this "handful" I gave up trying to know anything about Toledo. All I can say is that I was introduced to the town with much ceremony, and have an indefinite idea of its features, which are such a mixture of Goth, Moor, Jew, and Christian that, at the end of six hours, I suffered from as acute an indigestion as though I had swallowed an architectural mince-pie. If I lived in Toledo I should go mad. The conjunction of so much history, so much live art, and so much dead nature would set my brain on fire with conundrums. There is nothing more tragic than living among great things and little people. The very air is heavy with hopeless age, and stifles with every breath. I never felt so thankful for America as while walking through those narrow Toledan streets, every stone of which could tell tales of bloodshed and violence. The wildest Western settlement, populated with the most discouraging stumps, became in my eyes a far more tolerable home. Meditation belongs to the past, aspiration to the future. There is more hope in a pioneer's log-cabin than in all Toledo's monuments, and, platitude or no platitude, I must ask, What is life worth without hope? Time, that has reduced the "city of the Visigoths" from great riches to pauperism, may bring about a still more wondrous revolution, but Time's wheel turns slowly in dead latitudes. Before this change takes place, all Europe will be republican, Spain's deserts will become oases, and the

United States will be governed by its best and honestest brains.   After — the millennium!

A street in Toledo.

Touching both sides of the streets with my hands, I was first taken to a beautiful Moorish house, now the residence of a banker.   "Look," said the guide, and as I entered the great door I saw a modern carriage.   "It is the only carriage in town, Señora, and when the banker's family drive they go round and round the square." As the square is very small and exceedingly crowded, this dissipation in horse-flesh must be excessive. However, the satisfaction of doing what nobody else can afford may compensate for unparalleled monotony.

Not to admire Moorish architecture is to be incapable of appreciation. Its sad, solemn beauty and exquisite taste made me think of minor keys, and how truly Madame de Stael had called architecture "frozen music." Chopin's dreamiest nocturnes and reveries came into my head, and then harmony would be disturbed by contact with great Gothic pillars or portals. Thus it happened that all through the town my nerves were shocked by discords, — Goth and Jew rudely jostling the Moor, who alone preserved the dignity of repose, as if conscious of superior art. Through sight my ear was charmed one moment to be tortured the next, and I quickly found another reason for preferring the backwoods to Toledo. What musician can endure false notes? Thus tortured, I sympathized with Gautier and Irving in their lamentations over the downfall of the Moors. "For my part," says the Frenchman, "I've always regretted that the Moors did not remain masters of Spain, which has only lost by their expulsion." "They deserved this beautiful country," writes the American. "They won it bravely; they enjoyed it generously and kindly. . . . . I am at times almost ready to join in sentiment with a worthy friend and countryman of mine, whom I met in Malaga, who swears the Moors are the only people that ever deserved the country, and prays to heaven they may come over from Africa and conquer it again." Who knows but they may? Stranger things have happened; and why do the Moors jealously cherish the keys belonging to their old homes, if it be not with the hope of some time turning them in the rusty locks?

The queer turns, the sharp corners (now rounded) in the streets, were for what? For fighting. Ah, well, the world is not perfect, but, in spite of architecture and sculpture, I don't think it has retrograded. From ruin to ruin, from beggar to beggar, from church to church, we passed into the cathedral, two hundred and fifty years in building, costing the architect, Pedro Perez, fifty years of his life. What modern architect would give his existence to one work? Nothing but the patience of genius can so dedicate itself. Though very noble, there is much that is theatrical about the interior of the building. As in most Spanish cathedrals, the choir, being in the centre, destroys the grandeur of the *coup-d'œil.* The severe simplicity of the Cologne cathedral is infinitely more impressive, but I dared not say so, for Toledo is as dependent upon its cathedral as the play of "Hamlet" is upon the melancholy Dane.

Obstructive though it be, the choir is a marvel of ingenuity in itself, the three rows of wooden stalls carved by Philippe de Bourgogne et de Berrugnète being marvels of ingenuity. The art — Gothic bordering upon the Renaissance — cannot be called sacred, unless monkeys pursuing their own tails, and the strangest of unknown animals in the most ludicrous of poses, exhale a religious atmosphere ; but, as carving, it is irreproachable. While I sat in the archbishop's stall the custodian showed me a great gash on his head, received two years before, from two men, who felled him to the floor, bound him, and then robbed the church of jewels. They were afterwards arrested, recognized, and imprisoned.

"Ever since the blow I 've been deaf," said the custodian.

"Yes ; and when those rascals come out of prison they will kill you," rejoined my guide. "Better to have made no struggle and given no alarm. Your hearing will go from bad to worse."

The good-natured custodian shrugged his shoulders, and seemed content to have done his duty. How many victims to virtue are? Would the sacristan allow us to see the *custodia* of gilded silver with a *"richesse inouie"* of ornament, inlaid with diamonds and emeralds, costing three generations of artists a century's labor, the Virgin's mantle containing eighty-five thousand pearls?

" No," replied the sacristan, looking very hard at me. " A woman tried to steal some of the jewels recently."

I did not feel crushed by the imputation, because I knew a valuable *douceur* was what the sacristan wanted. I would not allow the Blinker to give it, and so I was a thief in disguise. How that sacristan scowled when we walked away, and how I wanted to devote those useless jewels to redeeming Toledo from dirt and ignorance !

In his "Handful" of Toledo, M. Parros de-
votes 745 pages to the cathedral.   Do you think
then that I dare touch an inexhaustible subject?
I will not even mention the Virgin Mary's appearance to St. Ildefonso, nor speak of a Toledan masterpiece, the Puerta del Sol, but will
ask you to gaze at a unique scene from the top
of the long-unfinished Alcazar, which stands on
the highest point of the town.   Toledo lay sleep-
ing at my feet, and the lazy Tagus wound around
it like a horseshoe.   Thankful that sight-seeing
was off my mind and legs, — six hours had all
three been tramping, — I gave myself up to the
quiet delight of breathing the soft, pure air that
fanned us.   It was a fine picture, — Toledo with
its quaint, gray towers, turrets, and cathedral
dome, and the naked russet hills that lost their
look of poverty and desolation in their reflected
glow of rich, warm sunshine.

"Is Toledo healthy?" I asked the guide.

"Not very, Señora. We have fevers because
we have no drainage, and the river is very low
and poisonous in summer. No one dares drink
it."

Politically Toledo is the Faubourg St. Germain
of Castile. Its brains, like its monuments, are in
ruins, and cling to the past, the dearest souvenir of which is Carlism. Still seeking my Republican, I thought he might be found in an intelligent guide, but the guide shook his head.

"No, Señora, I am a Carlist. Have you
remarked the deep gash on my face? That is
a trophy of which I am proud. I got it fighting for the Carlists. And there are other
wounds about my person. Now I'm too old
to fight. One of our principal citizens raised
a company of two hundred volunteers about ten
days ago and went off to join Don Carlos. They
did n't all leave at once, you know. The deed
was accomplished gradually, and the men wore

their ordinary clothes. But before starting the Carlists did us great service. The country about here had been infested with brigands. The Carlists planned an expedition and captured twenty-seven of them. Now we take long breaths. There are Carlists in disguise among the mountains here, acting as spies upon the government and upon brigands. Republicans will tell you that Carlists are bandits, but don't you believe it, Señora. They are gentlemen. We 've a fine lot of Republicans in Toledo. They threaten to destroy the town. What did they do a month ago but attempt to burn down our glorious cathedral ! Think of that ! But our best people heard of the plot, and frustrated it by surrounding the cathedral before the arrival of the incendiaries. They can't do that sort of thing, you know. We won't endure it."

"But surely these men are not Republicans

like Castelar. They do not support the government."

"No; they are Intransigentes. The government Republicans behave very well; only we don't like them. We want our King."

The setting sun warned us of the approaching train, and we sauntered back to the omnibus, taking *en route* an old curiosity-shop. There were Toledo blades made in Sheffield that I refused to buy, notwithstanding the Maid of Saragossa wrought upon the handles. I contented myself with bearing off a noble Moorish nail, and then learned how an appreciative Frenchman had recently bought several hundred of these unique nails with which to stud the great doors of his new Parisian hotel. Toledo is a paradise of *bric-à-brac.* When I make my fortune writing for newspapers, I shall follow the Frenchman's example, and, hitting the right nail on the head, ask for Moor !

How I enjoyed that return trip to Madrid! We were only three hours behind time, and the dinner-party I was to have joined at nine o'clock did coldly furnish forth a midnight supper-table, at which the guests were as conversational as blinking owls.

PART VII.

Last Day in Madrid.

VII.

A Disappointment. — A Model Banker. — Buying a Mantilla. — Seeing the Cortes. — Interview with Figueras. — A Carlist Nobleman. — Farewell to Madrid. — Giggling Nuns.

IT was my last day in Madrid, and President Castelar had offered to call at noon. "Too good to be true," I said, yet prepared for the best, by drawing up a series of questions that reduced Spain to a catechism. Twelve o'clock came and went, half past twelve, one o'clock, half past one, two o'clock, yet no Castelar, and no letter. He had forgotten the engagement, or he was ill, or he had sniffed that catechism afar off, and preferred breaking his word to facing its interrogations. I was extremely sorry, for, having

9

gone to Spain solely to see Castelar, it seemed a pity not to get beyond the cuticle of acquaintanceship; but one interview was all that I had reason to expect, and if he denied me the volunteered luxury of a second, I could not complain. There are women who never pardon a man's forgetfulness, though he carry state cares upon his shoulders. I put myself in Castelar's place, forgave him at two o'clock precisely, and then went in search of a banker. I found him in a quiet little office, where, in the brogue of an Irishman, I heard how he had known Washington Irving intimately; how charming Irving was; how he had met all the nice Americans visiting Spain. Then the banker, taking a singularly long time to sign his name to the necessary papers, gracefully referred to American women, and later glided upon the subject of Spain. He would not, could not believe in the permanency of the republic. The

Spaniards — he knew them well — were not im-
bued with self-sacrificing patriotism. What they
possessed was incarnate egotism. Mr. Banker
refused to modify his statements. I could get
no republicanism out of him, although I got
money on a letter of credit that he knew to be
worthless. He gave me gold without charging
the customary premium, and told me to be rid
of the bank-notes before leaving Madrid. The
Bank of Spain is not trusted outside of the
capital. A fine commentary on Peninsular
finances, is it not?

With money in my purse, I felt that I must
buy something Spanish, something that would
recall my wild chase after a republic, something
that I could hand down to posterity as a relic of
my Peninsular campaign. Spanish fans are now
made in France; in fact, the only bit of a woman's toilet not imported from France is the
mantilla, with which, according to some witty

Parisian, a woman must be as ugly as the three theological virtues in order not to be pretty.

When I went to call upon a pretty Spanish woman, she knew just how to buy a mantilla. "You must not go into a shop," she said. "Only foreigners do that, and get cheated. There are women merchants who go from house to house selling the property of ladies. The Spanish women are great traders. Even the rich sell their dresses when they tire of them, and now that times are hard there is a great deal of old lace in the market at reasonable rates. Many are disposing of real lace mantillas, and I can get you one cheap. The saleswoman will be here directly; but let me warn you against showing any eagerness about purchasing. Double the amount is asked that the woman will take, and your indifference will lead to a reduction of prices. Now remember."

In came the little old woman, and I remembered. With desire in my heart, but nonchalance in my manner, I turned Jew. I would give so much. The woman declared that the lady to whom the mantilla belonged would kill her if she

Bargaining for a mantilla.

did not obtain twice the sum. I laughed at the imposition. The little old woman delivered an oration to prove how, since the beginning of the world, there never had been anything so cheap.

I shrugged my shoulders. The little old woman held the mantilla before the light, that I might see the beauty of the rich black lace. She would part with the last hair on her head before she would take one real less for such a work of art. The north pole could not have melted less than I. O, very well then, the little old woman would go elsewhere. She would not basely sacrifice her client's property; and to my dismay I saw her pack up the mantillas and bid us good morning.

"Give yourself no concern," said the pretty, amiable Señora; "she will return. That is part of the play; and when she says you can have the mantilla for the price we named, give her an extra dollar for herself. It is always expected."

Truly enough, after making an excited exit, the little old woman returned, and, with a blandness that nothing but consummate schooling could have produced, presented the coveted mantilla. The gift of one dollar made the little old

woman beam with satisfaction, and, piling bene-
dictions upon my head, she left me mistress of
a real Spanish mantilla, which sober second
thought informed me was about as "handy to
have in the house" as Toodles's door-plate of
"Thompson with a p."

"Never mind," I whispered, coaxingly, to conscience; "it was cheap."

Conscience is very frank. Conscience is one
of those disagreeable friends that, for principle's
sake, always tells the truth. "Is anything you
do not want cheap at any price?"

I turned the conversation immediately.

'T is but a step from dress to politics, and I
took it. There stood a most obliging deputy
waiting to show us the Cortes. He thought
Spain in a bad way; he did not know what would
be the end of it; of course he hoped for the best.
He was *débonnair*, and looked as though he might
comfortably survive the loss of the republic; but

already I was becoming accustomed to the Spanish happy-go-lucky way of treating revolutions.
One thing the kindly deputy did know, that
Castelar was ill in bed with one of his bilious
headaches, and could not see any of the government until late in the afternoon. This, then,
accounted for Castelar's broken promise to me,
and I was doubly sorry.

There is nothing remarkable about the Spanish
Cortes. Plain externally, it has numerous well-
furnished committee-rooms, containing modern
portraits and paintings of no artistic value, while
its Chamber of Deputies, arranged like an amphitheatre, is remarkable for nothing but its deeds.
The Bourbon crown, the Queen's portrait, have
been removed, but the great doors by which Her
Majesty used to enter have never been thrown
open to the President. The odor of royalty still
clings to the Cortes.

"Are you a well-behaved body?" I asked.

The good-natured deputy smiled, and the amiable señora replied, "Well behaved? They act like children. They exercise no self-control. You never in your life heard such a noise as they make. And then how they use up carpets! Spit, spit, spit! They are forever spitting; and what would happen to a woman's skirts if she came upon the floor, I leave you to imagine."

"Did the rain of expectoration set in with the reign of the republic?"

"O no. It has always been. I see no difference."

Here was a revelation. The noble art of spitting is not confined to the Western Hemisphere. It is not peculiar to republican institutions. I breathe more freely. Shakespeare's Rosalind declares that "very good orators, when they are out, they will spit." This was centuries ago, so perhaps, after all, it is the noble gift of oratory with

9 *

which our country is blessed that induces a less pleasing deluge.

. Once more at my hotel, I had begun to pack my bundle, when Señor Figueras, then President of the Cortes, was announced. I made the acquaintance of a tall, dark, affable, courteous, enlightened gentleman, a lawyer by profession, a republican from conviction. He welcomed me to Spain, because I was an American; he spoke of his own country calmly. He thought the republic would succeed, not because there were so many republicans, but because there were seven monarchical parties opposed to one another, all of which preferred the republic to the triumph of any other enemy. That very day an Alphonsist general had frankly avowed the impossibility of putting Alphonso on the throne for several years. "Let the republic endure several years," added Señor Figueras, "and the monarchy can have no chance. It is the present that concerns us.

But whether the republic endures or not, Cuban slavery is doomed. Spain is committed to abolition, and cannot imperil her honor."

If all Spain were made up of Castelars and Figuerases, certainly not; but has Spain never said one thing and done another?

Señor Figueras stated that the bourgeois class was not republican. Señor Castelar had, to my amazement, maintained the reverse. In the disagreement of doctors, I followed my own observation, and believed Señor Figueras. Shopkeepers rarely rise above their pockets. The President of the Cortes saw a brilliant future for Spain. She was the richest country in Europe; she possessed enormous wealth in unworked mines; she had great possibilities in grain; her flour was the finest in the world. All would come with good government, education, skilled labor, and railroads. Ay, verily, Señor Figueras. Spain's redemption is a mere question of time, but how

long a time? Then I was told that Spain had no
Finance Minister, no General, and that the army
officers were monarchists.

"In the name of all that is possible, how can
you make headway against an empty treasury,
no commander, and lukewarm officers?" I asked.
"Does not this account for the prolonged resist-
ance of Carlists and Intransigentes?"

Señor Figueras shrugged his shoulders, but
smiled hopefully. He had faith in his cause,
knew that it must succeed sooner or later, and
was willing to sacrifice himself to it. If, like
Sodom, the Spanish republic can be saved by one
honest man, there need be no fear.

The republic has no military leader, while
there are six generals and one hundred and fifty
brigadier-generals in Spain. What a commentary!

It was growing dark; even Spanish trains start
some time, and I was forced to bid Señor Figueras

farewell much sooner than I wished. He hoped
to visit America; perhaps he would "assist" at
our Centennial celebration. Until then — And
when the door closed I said to my doubting self,
"Spain is not to be despised when she can give
birth to a Castelar and a Figueras. Other sons
may be nobler than I think, and her daughters
may only require opportunity to exhibit the finest
womanly traits."

I had asked to see an eminently respectable
Spaniard who actually believed in Don Carlos,
and one of the kindest-hearted Americans that
ever lived thirty years away from home served
a Carlist for my dessert at dinner. He was a
nobleman, good-natured, fat, utterly incapable of
mental or physical exertion, and said little. The
contrast between him and the republicans was
so marked that I again took my doubting self
into a corner and whispered, " If intelligence wins
in the long run, the republicans, though they

be one to one hundred, must gain the victory." The ponderous way in which that Carlist sat down on everything, and did not realize his own absurdity, amazed me more than the Escorial itself; for the Escorial is as dead as Death, while this Carlist was alive, read a newspaper occasionally, and could listen, if he would, to Castelar's thrilling orations.

The hour of bills and farewells at last arrived, and it is hard to say which was the more touched, — heart or pocket. Madrid is not the poor travellers' paradise. Living is higher than in any other European capital, and the American system of charging for meals, whether eaten or not, makes sad inroads upon the purse. The Blinker was in his element. Every waiter seemed to be his bosom friend, and his lavish generosity in fees affected me deeply. Our departure was profoundly regretted in consequence, and as we drove away I found myself moralizing on the superiority of money over other virtues. It is always appreciated. No ghost need rise from the grave to proclaim its transcendent merits. It makes the hideous beautiful, the foolish wise, the stupid witty, and the wicked saints. It can patronize genius, and dictate to nations. It is very fine to be Shakespeare after death, but how much more comfortable to be Rothschild while living! Is the applause of posterity a satisfactory equivalent for present cakes and ale?

I had dispensed with the brilliant Blinker during my stay in Madrid; consequently existence had been unruffled. Of course the moment I needed him he was found wanting. It is something always to realize expectations. No sooner had we arrived at the station than the Blinker succeeded in quarrelling with an official about his carpet-bag. It was enlivening to see two men pulling one small carpet-bag two ways, while addressing endearing epithets to each other; and, after fully enjoying the spectacle, I demanded an explanation.

Tussle for a carpet-bag.

"Madam," said the Blinker, who by this time had tugged himself into a violent perspiration and displayed to an admiring audience the one pocket-handkerchief with which he had come into Spain, — "madam, I wish my carpet-bag to go as luggage, and they say here it cannot."

"For what reason?"

"Because I bought the tickets in town, and

when tickets are bought away from the station, passengers must take their luggage with them or go without."

"Certainly, and that's as it should be. Yet this man is attempting to defy our rules," added the indignant official.

How I could have laughed, but I refrained. "I never heard such an idiotic regulation," I said to the panting official.

The Blinker looked pleased.

"There is but one thing more idiotic," I added, turning to him, "which is that you who have lived twenty-six years in Spain should not have known what you were about."

The Blinker looked less pleased.

Think what a state I should have been in had not my trunk been a bundle! We could not have departed without buying a third ticket.

Intending to travel all night, I entered the compartment for *Dames Seules,* and met there

N

one of the señoras I had journeyed with from Santander to Madrid. Curiosity sat upon her tongue, and I was thoroughly interviewed. The señora had never visited Toledo, and had only seen the Escorial from the railroad. Would I tell her about them? So an American five days in Madrid found herself expounding Spain to a native! The native was *naïve* in her ignorance, and when I had answered all her questions, she exclaimed, " How strangely American women must feel! If they know so much, how wonderful the men must be!" At this moment the rest of the compartment was taken possession of by a frolicsome party of nuns, who, when the train started, paused in their chattering to cross themselves, and then babbled on as ceaselessly as a mountain-brook, — one moment in French and the next in Spanish. It was the youngest conversation I ever listened to, and I wondered whether getting to a nunnery made children of mature women. Like school-girls, these giggling nuns jumped out of the train at midnight, followed by my acquaintance and her maid, and until seven o'clock the next morning I was monarch of the most uncomfortable compartment in which a woman never slept a wink.

PART VIII.

Crossing the Frontier.

VIII.

A FEW miles west of Saragossa we changed our train, the Blinker appearing with his carpet-bag, intensely disgusted that all the beggars were still asleep, — a criminal offence, which obliged him to be his own porter. Again I was the sole occupant of a dirty compartment that consoled me for not being pecuniarily interested in Spanish railroads. Again I gazed upon sunburnt desolation, and when we stopped at a station, situated in the middle of nothing, there was a tumultuous appearance of nobody that made me tremble for dividends. However, I did see an officer get out at an impossible place, and be received by the entire population, consisting of four women, six men, and a boy. He had evidently returned from the war, and was embraced with such disregard of spectators as gave me an appetite for the breakfast I was not to eat. His wife threw her arms about his neck, laughing with all the joy of her impulsive heart, the little boy clung to his father's legs and screamed in Spanish, the father's father felt of his son to see whether he really had come back all in one piece, while three women and five men slapped the hero on his back and shouted a hearty welcome. I may be mistaken about the relations existing between these happy people, but, if they were not as I imagine, they ought to have been.

Gradually we approached the Carlist region, and at ten o'clock stopped at a station where soldiers stood at ease and crowds of men were lounging.

The break in the railroad was not far off. How to secure a conveyance after arriving at Tafalla, no one in Madrid had been able to tell me. So, as the Blinker condescended to ask whether I wanted anything, I desired him to inquire about diligences and telegraph to Tafalla for places.

"Perfectly useless," replied he who had lived twenty-six years in Spain; "no one can give any information here, and who knows whether a telegram will be sent ?"

In the language of Sheridan Knowles's Julia, I tragically exclaimed, "Do it, nor leave the task to me."

The Blinker suddenly vanished, and there appeared an exceedingly polite official, who, in good French, offered to assist me, a stranger, by securing seats in the diligence from Tafalla to Pampeluna. "The agency is here," he added, "and you will have no chance unless you apply immediately." Well, that Blinker returned soon after,

10

nodded smilingly, exhibited tickets for the diligence, and looked as though he had gained a victory over me by successfully doing what I had pronounced impossible. In six months he would have ruined the temper of Griselda.

We were in the Province of Navarre, and as we crossed the bridge thrown over the river Aragon, guarded on both banks by Republican soldiers, I began to scent the not distant Carlists. They dared not go beyond the Aragon for fear of ambuscades, and the bridge was protected lest the enemy should attempt to blow it up. On arriving at Tafalla, a town of five thousand inhabitants, once called "la flor de Navarre" (the flower of Navarre), and long the residence of its kings, the railroad came to an end. Beyond lay wreck and bullets. Planting my feet on *terra incognita*, I sent the Blinker in advance, that his burly form might cut a passage through soldiers, civilians, boys, and officials, packed like herrings, and no more dis-

posed to make way for a woman than if I'd been
Don Carlos. Once on the other side of the station, I looked in vain for the diligence. "What
does this mean?" I asked the Blinker.

"There is no diligence. We must go to Pampeluna in an omnibus."

Before me stood the omnibus. It was dirty,
rickety, narrow, intended for eight inside and nobody knows how many outside. I secured a seat
by the door, and to my amazement the Blinker
took the one opposite, instead of mounting beside
the driver. I could no more have ordered him
outside than I could have asked Jeremy Diddler
for the loan of money ingeniously abstracted from
my own person. There are forms of impudence
that paralyze the tongue and render limp the
muscles. To face the Blinker for six weary hours
seemed more than flesh and spirit could endure.
Still, I had heard of people retiring within themselves, and I was about to attempt this feat when

the other passengers appeared. There was a smiling woman with a caged parrot; the woman's husband, carrying a deeply tragic baby; a very fat woman, with a fat boy and a fatter bandbox; a dark young man, much given to staring; and last, yet most unique of all, a gigantic Spanish peasant without stockings, and with a constitutional disregard for shirt-bosom that proved him superior to the etiquette of dress. There were rings in his ears, and he grasped in his right hand a huge staff, with which he could have laid us low — omnibus and all — in less time than confirmed stutterers require to pronounce the historic name of Jack Robinson.

Entering the omnibus on the double-quick, the Brigand — for such he would have been on the stage — landed in the Blinker's lap, much to the Blinker's disgust.

"Madam," said my protector, extricating himself as best he could, "I will go outside. You will then have more space."

I blessed that Brigand, who grunted intense
satisfaction at the decision, and planted his staff
on the toes of the staring young man. The latter
jumped up suddenly, and vented his agony in a
suppressed howl. Seeing matters take a lively
turn, the parrot began to talk, and, I grieve to
say, swore roundly in Spanish. The tragic baby
scowled at the profane bird, the boy put his fingers through the cage and got well bitten, at
which he cried bitterly, and was shaken by his
mother, whose bandbox he had kicked disrespect-
fully. The entire performance so amused the
Brigand that he laughed prodigiously, and addressed me in a patois as incomprehensible as
Koptic. When I shook my head at him the
Brigand laughed louder than ever, and a deep
scar, running the entire length of his forehead,
grew fearfully red. It was an animal that I saw
before me, a creature of impulse and passion, good-
natured until angered, and then a fiend. With

all his diabolic possibilities I preferred his company to the Blinker's.

There is dust and dust, and Spain is the mother of all dust. It is the whitest, lightest, heaviest, stickiest dust on earth. It enveloped us in clouds; it flew at us as though possessed of wings. A broiling sun poured upon my back; the dust poured into my ears, up my nose, and down my throat. In desperation we closed the windows and gasped for breath. Without, there was nothing but dust and desolation. We were in the region of Carlists. Telegraph wires dragged upon the ground, railroad bridges were blown up, and solitary stations were torn inside out. But where was the enemy? Not to have seen a Carlist would be to have lived in vain, and I was beginning to pine for one, when a very dirty, ragged man with a gun, followed by several ragged boys, suddenly appeared in front of the omnibus and commanded the driver to halt.

We stopped.

It was the enemy.

Seven men, three women, a boy, a baby, and a parrot, surrendered to one man and a gun.

Meeting the Carlists.

The enemy disappointed me sadly. He did not throw open the omnibus door, exclaiming, "Your money or your life!" He neither relieved me of my watch nor frantically tore the rings from my fingers. In fact, he scorned to look at one of us. He confined his parley to the driver, and, after exacting the toll which all must pay, allowed us to continue our journey. And I had left my jewelry in France! It was humiliating.

Twice I descried small groups of men, attired in dust-colored rags, and leaning against stone-walls. They were the mighty enemy, and again we stopped to pay toll to an army of one.

Unmolested, we entered the walled garrison town of Pampeluna, and, rattling through its very noble and loyal streets, stopped before the Fonda del Infante in the Paseo de Valencia. From gazing upon one Carlist I gazed upon regiments of Republicans. Why the regiments did not sally forth and annihilate the one Carlist seemed queer; but fighting in Spain is queer.

It was five o'clock in the afternoon, and I had had nothing to eat but a few grapes since the

night before. It occurred to me that, being in
front of a real hotel, I might have a real dinner;
"but before ordering it, or even securing a room,
find out the hour of departure for Bayonne," I
said to the Blinker, who shook hands with everybody, and seemed to be on terms of intimacy with
the entire town.

"Madam, we will start to-morrow morning at
seven, and you shall have your dinner in half an
hour," he replied, leading me to a room in which
ablution seemed possible.

The dust, which had made my clothing and hair
as white as a miller's, had made my face black.
My appearance was an insult to a cracked look-
ing-glass. Emerging from my disguise, I lay
down to snatch a few minutes' repose, but was
aroused by a violent rattling of the door-latch.

"Madam," shouted the well-known voice, "get
ready to depart at once. The troops have received orders to march on the enemy to-morrow

10   o

at daybreak. As soon as they leave the gates of the town will be shut. No one will be able to get out or in; and the Governor says we must start this evening. The diligence is now ready."

Why had not that exasperating courier made inquiries before engaging a room and ordering dinner? Because he wanted me to pay for lodging and food that I did not have, I suppose. Hurrying from the hotel, rushing through squares alive with troops, we entered a dark, dingy street where stood an empty omnibus. That was the diligence.

"Where are the horses?" I asked. "You told me the conveyance was ready."

"Well, they said so," responded the Blinker; "but the driver," pointing to a thin, cunning-looking man leaning against a wall, "says we shall not go for an hour."

And I had been cheated out of my real dinner.

"I am famished. Buy me something to eat."

The Blinker soon returned with a huge piece of bread, and, seated in a stable doorway on my property, I proceeded to munch and munch and munch, while mounted orderlies dashed to

A dinner extraordinary.

and fro, wretched ambulance and baggage wagons passed by, and the dirtiest soldiers I ever beheld — Carlists excepted — stood about in groups, smoking and laughing. All were young, and all looked as though they had as much idea of discipline as a monkey has of the theory of evolution. They were a mob in uniform.

"Ask those soldiers nearest whether they are republicans," I said to the Blinker, who reluctantly obeyed.

From birth the Blinker had been opposed to information, and interpreted with the intelligence of an idiot. He generally forgot the point of everything, and substituted "chose." Nothing could have been more lucid. The soldiers, however, did not tax his intellect severely. They merely shrugged their shoulders, and made the situation particularly agreeable by watching every mouthful I ate, and inviting me to join the army and become their *vivandière.* "Live the vivandière!" they shouted in chorus. Not knowing what would happen next, I retreated to the omnibus, after telling the driver, in original and furious pantomime, that if he did not harness his horses immediately, I should not go at all. Much to my astonishment, that pantomime produced an effect. The driver disappeared, returned with his horses, and in a short time the Blinker and I, sole passengers, were driven out of Pampeluna.

Were we to travel all night? No. In about an hour's time we stopped suddenly before an isolated, dirty stone building. It was what is known in Spain as a *posada* (resting-place), the peculiarity of such a public house being that it offers entertainment for both man and beast; beast ranging over the ground-floor, and man having the floor above. Posadas are mostly patronized by drovers and tramps, so that accommodations are limited to bed and board; nevertheless, I was thankful to escape being shut up in Pampeluna, and accepted my lodging without a murmur. Conducted to the only tolerable bedroom, I frightened my hostess by throwing open the windows.

"What do you do that for?" she asked.

"To breathe some fresh air. I am stifled."

The room seemed never to have been ventilated; but then, what it lacked in ventilation was made up in perfume. Stables may be healthy, but their stale aroma hardly recommends itself to a cultivated nose.

"How very strange to like fresh air!" exclaimed the hostess. "Are you not afraid of it? These are busy times. We always put several people in this room. You won't object to having some one occupy the second bed?"

Object? Would n't I, though? I 'd leave the house, I 'd sit up in the omnibus, I 'd — But it was unnecessary to threaten further, for mine hostess gave up her idea as soon as she saw I would not be imposed upon. Posada or palace, human nature is ever the same, bullying where it may, and cringing where it must.

Would I have dinner? Would n't I? The

hostess set the table in my room, disappeared,
and soon returned with a tureen. Sitting in
solitary barrenness, gazing at this tureen by the
light of the sickliest tallow-candle I ever snuffed,
I wondered what was within. Its contents were
novel to the eye, and hardly inviting to the appetite. Too thick to be called soup, it was not solid
enough to be considered anything else in English.
It had as many colors as Spain has politics.
Perhaps it was a boiled kaleidoscope. It seemed
to have the jaundice, yet it was white in streaks,
and was illuminated with red polka-spots. Could
it be the national *olla podrida ?* It is the first
mouthful that costs, and, screwing my courage
to the sticking-place, I tasted. Imagine stale egg
combined with stewed oil, and you have a vivid
idea of what I swallowed. My first mouthful was
my last, and when mine hostess entered with the
second service she expressed surprise at the small-
ness of my appetite.

"Everybody always eats here," she said, and left me to ruminate. The dish before me was Spanish ham, cut very thick, russet-colored, very bulgy in the middle, and, viewed geographically, looked like the top slice off a sierra. With undaunted bravery I took a discreet bite. That ham was salt enough to have preserved the republic, had it fed on it instead of hope.

Covering the retreat of that undulating edible with sour bread, I called aloud for the Blinker. He appeared with his mouth full. Of course he could eat. Misery likes company, but even in the capacity of sympathizer the Blinker was a failure.

"The dinner is detestable. I can touch nothing."

"What does madam expect? I find it very good."

"I expect you to get me some grapes. On leaving Madrid you overruled my order for a box of fruit, by assuring me that we should pass through a grape region. With grapes I can exist. Buy me six pounds."

"Bien, madame."

In half an hour the Blinker returned, again with his mouth full, saying that it was impossible to obtain any grapes; none grew in the neighborhood.

"Then why did you not obey my order in Madrid?"

"Madam, I have lived twenty-six years in Spain —"

"Enough. Leave the room."

The Blinker departed smilingly. Going to the open window, I feasted upon the gloriously bright stars of a gloriously clear Spanish night. I was hungry enough to have eaten the Little Bear roasted, and thirsty enough to have drunk out of the Dipper; but I did neither. How little credit we receive for our most heroic self-denial!

Star by star,

Near and far,

Throbbed with hallowed light,

Whispering me,

"Sleep, for we

Watch through all the night."

It was very nice in the stars to soothe my nerves and talk so confidentially, but would they wake me if beetle-browed bandits, enveloped in the mantle sacred to dark deeds, came through the floor or the ceiling, and with a dagger in one hand and a lantern in the other familiarly laughed, "Ha! ha!" and stabbed me through the heart? I was quite ready to give up my letter of credit; but if bandits were familiar with "panics," would this satisfy them? At least I would leave the window open, so that the stars might have the opportunity of being as good as their word; and, indeed, it was a comfort to catch their eye, for I discovered a panel door at the head of my bed, and my tallow-candle expired after a short and fitful existence. Clutching a match-box, I shut my eyes and awaited my fate. It came not in the shape of bandits, but of a *charivari* from the guests occupying the ground-floor. It sounded like a nightmare, but it was principally a donkey, assisted at intervals by a chorus of pigs, and so fiendish as to excite the indignation of a neighboring watch-dog. If there be any noise more unearthly than the braying of a donkey I have yet to hear it. The shrill yell of an ill-tempered locomotive is a penny whistle by comparison. There is so much more bray than there is donkey that the human intellect becomes hopelessly bewildered in endeavoring to solve the mystery. Lost in its cavernous depths, I had totally forgotten bandits, when the Blinker's tenor voice piped forth the fact that it was two o'clock in the morning, and would I please remember the omnibus started in fifteen minutes. For the first time I dressed by the light of matches, — a performance requiring considerable sleight of hand. Having nearly set fire to myself by holding them in my fingers, I finally stacked them as soldiers stack bayonets, and completed an original toilet. I felt one-sided for twenty-four hours. Then, igniting the match-box, I illuminated my way down precipitate stone steps into the omnibus.

What a strange drive it was! Beyond the posada everything was asleep but the stars, that still held their vigils, yet blinked more frequently, I fancied, as if quite ready to be relieved. Not a vehicle passed us, but ever and anon we stopped at solitary houses, where we evidently were expected, for men came out with lanterns, handed small bundles to the driver, and talked in a low tone. Then off we went again, without additional passengers.

"This is very queer," I said to the Blinker.

"How did these people know we should pass before daylight? The regular hour of departure from Pampeluna is seven o'clock. Yet people are up and waiting for us."

"Madam, do you suppose it would pay to run this omnibus from Pampeluna to Bayonne for two passengers? Not at all. It carries contraband goods, and the men who supply the bundles are smugglers. The drivers know how to manage. They are great friends with the frontier officers."

I was consorting with smugglers! The sensation was novel, and I began to feel like the heroine in a melodrama who innocently assists at the plotting of heavy villains. When we next stopped I left the vehicle to inspect the smugglers, and found them no worse looking than other people, one of them being so polite as to drink my health in the cognac I had refused. On learning my nationality, he declared he should

go to my country, for Spain was growing so poor
that an honest man could n't live even by stealing !

Was Mr. Smuggler a republican ?

Mr. Smuggler laughed. " My politics are a
little of all (*un poco de todas*). This, you see,
is very convenient. Whichever party comes up
I agree with, and so I keep my temper, and make
money whenever I get a chance."

I never saw a happier-looking man than Mr.
Smuggler. It is a great mistake to think good
people the most light-hearted and contented.
They are bothered by conscience and worried
about everlasting damnation. This world is most
enjoyed by airy sinners clever enough to escape
detection.

At dawn a third passenger joined us, a Spaniard, looking very cross, and quite as cross as he
looked. I did not blame him, for the only time
he opened his mouth he informed us that he was
being ruined by the civil war.

"I've been in the habit of carrying grain into France. I've horses and wagons for the purpose. Now my trade is completely ruined. If I attempt to cross the frontier, the Carlists seize my grain. I'm going to Bayonne to tell the merchants I must give up business." After this outburst the retiring trader glared savagely at nothing in particular.

Of course I inquired anxiously about his political creed, and was answered thus: "I am tired of civil war. People of the industrial classes are desperate. We'll accept any government that restores order."

As the morning grew older the scenery became less monotonous, such as could be seen through the dust, and peasants of both sexes were occasionally passed or overtaken. All of them seemed to be intimately acquainted with the driver, who, when the pedestrians were going our way, slackened speed sufficiently for them to dash into the omnibus and take boisterous possession of the vacant seats. The younger men stood on the steps, and while embracing the door puffed tobacco-smoke in my face; none of these impromptu passengers ever paid a real. They bounced out as unceremoniously as they dashed in, screamed at the driver as long as he was within ear-shot, and appeared to be as happy as though they read and wrote and attended lectures once a week.

Soon began the ascent of the Spanish Pyrenees, that noble mountain-range dividing the Peninsula from France. What happy hits Nature makes in her boundaries! They are absolute inspirations. With the Pyrenees came little old towns, the houses of which were adorned with imposing armorial bearings, last remnants of the old aristocratic vanity. Entering the beautiful Valley of Baztan, we passed over historic ground. Here in 1813 the French and English fought hand to

hand; here in 1834 Don Carlos the Pretender
penetrated into Spain; here, five years later, he
retired into France; and here to-day's Carlists
roam at sweet will, doing what they please,
merely because nobody tells them they shall not.
They are in their stronghold. Always independent,
always forming a species of republic, this Basque
province has ever preserved its hatred of Spanish
centralization,— a hatred Carlism knows well how
to turn to account. Baztan is but a transposition of
the Basque word *baznat*, signifying " I am alone,"
— a true expression of its people's dominant
characteristic. They are alone, too, in the beauty
of their landscape. These fierce egotists. need
only look out of their windows to behold a tall
mountain-range on the right, a superb carriage-
road winding round it, a rich laughing valley below, — scenery for a glimpse of which less favored
mortals journey hundreds of miles. Some day
when they have sense enough to appreciate the

advantages of reading and writing Spanish, and prefer to be part of a nation to the whole of a province, these Baztanians will repudiate Carlism. That time has not yet come.

We were approaching the frontier, and I began to be nervous about Carlists, not from fear of meeting them, but from fear of the reverse. Ever on the watch for the enemy, I yet failed to notice a pedestrian until he had lightly tripped into the omnibus and seated himself opposite me. He was young, good-looking, obstinate, — just such a fellow as a theatrical manager would prize for leader of a supernumerary army in a spectacle destined to run one hundred nights. He was clothed in dusty brown linen. He carried a demoralized-looking knapsack and a gun. On his breast was a worsted heart, emblem of the sacred heart of Jesus; and on his head he wore the white cap of the country, generally adopted by the Carlists, on which was embroidered in gold,

"God, King, and Country. Live Carlos VII.!"
When asked to exhibit his cap, the defender of
Divine Right did so willingly, but not one word
would he utter, making up for paucity of conversation by the steadiest of stares, which lasted
until it pleased him to jump out of the omnibus,
— of course without paying, — and take to the
woods. As he prepared to leave I offered him
the remains of a bottle of cognac, and the uncivil
creature refused it, perhaps because he took me
for a Spaniard. Spaniards never intend you to
accept their presents. They enjoy all the glory
of giving with none of the expense.

Before the silent Carlist's departure, the omnibus halted, and two lusty young men clambered
up beside the driver. Shortly after his disappearance, a boy on horseback suddenly emerged
from I don't know where. Again the omnibus
stopped, one of the young men jumped down,
shook hands with the boy, received from him a

package and a stout walking-stick, returned, and
we once more pursued our precipitate, winding
way. Just before reaching the Spanish frontier,
which is headquarters for a band of Carlists, these
two youths jumped from the omnibus and retired
precipitately to the woods. Evidently there was
something the matter, but whether they were
escaped murderers or spies, or worse, I could not
imagine. Whatever their crime, they were aided
and abetted by our omnibus driver, who, ten
minutes afterward, hobnobbed with Carlists as
cordially as he had consorted with Republicans
at Pampeluna. Smugglers have no country.

At last I was gratified by the sight of Carlist
officers in clean clothes. Stopping in front of
their headquarters, — a posada commanding the
road, — we were surrounded by a number of
handsome boys in the becoming Hussar uniform.
Out of the windows hung others, equally young
and equally well dressed. They were in striking

contrast to the ragged creatures previously encountered, and looked like gentlemen, the sons
of old Carlist families enthusiastic in defence of
their cause. Most of them wore the sacred heart
of Jesus, and all conducted themselves with perfect propriety. I saw but one gray-haired officer.
He it was who inspected the passports of our two
male passengers, waiving the ceremony in my
case, and exacted tribute of the driver. From
the posada flaunted a beautiful Spanish flag,
evidently new, on which was inscribed, "God,
King, and Country," below the arms of Carlos
VII., surmounted by the Virgin Mary holding
the sacred heart in her hand. There was such
a picnicky, only-pretending, meaning-no-gunpow-
der air about these jaunty Carlists that, if I 'd
had a trustworthy courier, I 'd have remained
several hours, "interviewed" them, and made
the rest of the journey in a private carriage.
With a Blinker, what could I do but stifle my

inclination ?   Only a journalist knows what agony
I endured in throwing away such exceptional
material.   None but a journalist appreciates my
self-restraint in not strangling the Blinker.

Leaving the posada, we were stopped for a
second Carlist inspection, and in a moment after
stood on French ground in the presence of French
bayonets.   The contrast between the red baggy-
pantalooned, long blue-coated Gauls and their
pretty neighbors was most amusing.   The former
meant business and the latter play.

"What do you think of those Carlists?" I
asked the weather-beaten officer to whose keen-
eyed scrutiny we were subjected.

"We pay no attention to them," he answered,
with a contemptuous expression of mouth.   "We
mind our own affairs.   All I know is that they
raised a new flag the other day and got *joliment
gris* (prettily drunk)."

This was all I could extract from the Frenchman.

Having crossed both frontiers, our journey now became uninteresting; at least it would have been so had not those two escaped murderers again appeared. Quickly emerging from some bushes, they tumbled into the omnibus, pulled up all the windows, and, without explanation, lay down upon the seats, totally regardless of me or anybody else.

"Upon my word," I exclaimed indignantly, "this is about the most brazen performance I ever witnessed. Shutting all the windows, too, without asking permission. I shall stifle." And down went the windows near me.

No sooner had I let in a breath of fresh air than the youth on my side raised the glass. I lowered it, only to see him again close it. This was too much. Turning to the Blinker, I said: "If you 've the spirit of the ninth part of a man, you 'll ask these intruders what they mean by such impertinence."

"Bien, madame," responded the Blinker calmly, and then the youths condescended to explain.

They were running away from the Spanish conscription. They did n't want to fight on either side. They did n't believe in either. Like Mercutio, they were ready to exclaim, "A plague on both your houses!" The boy on horseback had brought them letters and money. The driver was a friend. By taking to the woods they had escaped arrest at the frontier. Our long delay at the French station was in order to give them time to cross the country. We should soon pass through a French town, and they wanted to avoid the *gens d'armes.* This was why they wished the windows closed. They intended to sail for Monte Video the next day, if the *gens d'armes* did not seize them.

It was astounding how quickly my wrath subsided, and how willingly I inhaled the vilest atmosphere. Covering the runaways with my cloak,

I forced them to keep their heads down, for they were perpetually bobbing up to see if the *gens d'armes* were looking. We passed through the town without interruption, and on reaching the suburbs the youths resumed their tramp over untravelled country. When last I saw them they were gleefully waving their caps, shouting, "To America!"

Shall I ever make another such journey? In one long, dusty day I had consorted with smugglers, Carlists, and escaped conscripts!

PART IX.

Last Day of All.

IX.

OUR last day's journey began at two o'clock in the morning. It was seven o'clock in the evening when, lumbering over the Allées Marines, we entered the fortress of Bayonne (Basque, *Baia una,* a port), whence comes the word *Bayonnette,* for in early times the men of Bayonne were famed as armorers. During the end of the sixteenth or beginning of the seventeenth century, a Basque regiment opposed to Spaniards in the Rhune Mountain ran short of ammunition, and, sticking the long knives commonly carried by them into the barrels of their muskets, charged the enemy. The scene of action has ever since been called La Bayonnette, and from that murderous inspiration sprang the more civilized though no less effective bayonet, without which the Zouave's occupation would be gone.

We came to a final halt in a small square, dominated by a tall, gray hostelry, the windows of which were alive with heads belonging to serving-maids, evidently off duty, for they chattered like a wilderness of monkeys, or the House of Commons when the majority want to talk down a hated opponent.

"At what hotel shall we stop?" I asked the Blinker.

"This one," he replied, ordering the removal of the luggage.

The Blinker was once more on his native heath, and every one of those female heads nodded to him, as if to say, "Won't we all dine together,

and won't we make you tell us about Spain?"
And in my mind's eye I saw the Blinker swelling
visibly as he painted his own heroic exploits and
my American imbecility.

"Ah, my fine gentleman, you want me to stop
at this fourth-rate inn because you'll meet your
long-lost own, do you?" quoth I to myself.
"Well, I won't." Then, turning suddenly, I said
we would go to the Hôtel de Commerce.

"Mais, madame, it is some distance. There
are bags and bundles. This is convenient —"

"Very, for you. My convenience is of another
color. Do as I say."

"Bien, madame." The Blinker smiled. Inter-
cepting a hand-car, into which our impedimenta
were stowed, we began our march, much to the
disgust of the female heads.

It was not an imposing procession.

HAND-CAR.
THE BLINKER.
MYSELF.

Had it been my aim to impress the inhabitants of Bayonne with either my beauty or my impor-

"It was not an imposing procession."

tance, I should have failed; for I looked like an ambulating dust-bin, and my bags resembled recent Pompeian excavations. But in France who cares for appearance? Its glory is exceeding social toleration; and until we learn to mind our own business, and let our neighbors cultivate their eccentricities to the top of their bent, we shall have a very important lesson to learn of despised Gaul. "O France, France," I inwardly exclaimed, in sitting down to a comfortable dinner at the table d'hôte, "with all thy faults I love thee still. Heaven be praised for thee! Confound the narrow souls who would polish thee off the face of the earth! Without thee we should have no *cuisine*, no cooks, no names for new dishes, no Lyonnaise potatoes, no Bordeaux, no Burgundy, no French bread, no coffee, no Sèvres china, no Lyons silks, no dressmakers, no fashions, no bonnets, no decent gloves, no bonbons, no Alfred de Musset, no Victor Hugo, no George Sand, no *Revue des Deux Mondes,* no school of acting, no plays to steal from, no live school of painting, no language to say nothing in beautifully, no Bon Marché, no articles of vertu, no revolutions, no Commune, no Paris to go to when we are good and die young! Salut à la France!"

Q

And, waving an imaginary tricolor in my left hand, I took soup with my right. After that nasty Spanish mess it tasted like the chosen food of the gods. Adam's first bite at the first apple had not more flavor.

I had sent the Blinker in search of the trunk, which had been attacked by cholera at Santander. He appeared in the middle of dinner to say that it had not arrived. Here was an unexpected blow, and, of course, the moment my table companions learned I had been to Spain, the flood-gates of conversation opened. "Ah," said the little thin man at my left, "I've visited Santander. A fine state they are in,—just like them to keep your trunk."

"It's a great trial having Spain so near," muttered a Frenchman opposite. "Always in a state of revolution!" You would have supposed that France had never fought a battle.

"You sympathize with the Republicans?" asked a third Frenchman.

"O yes. An American can do no less, and what I saw of the Carlists did not prepossess me in their favor. I saw nothing but rags and boys."

"Do I look like a boy?" thundered a tall, broad-shouldered, good-looking, blond young man at the other end of the table. He spoke English, yet did not impress me as English, and there was something in his accent and manner that seemed un-American. Puzzled, I replied, "Far from it."

"Well, I'm a Carlist."

"Indeed? Had the small boys I met on the frontier resembled you, I should have called them stalwart soldiers."

This unexpected *douceur* somewhat mitigated the rising anger of the unknown Carlist, who was bursting with importance and wanted to air his opinions upon at least a thousand persons. "That man ought to be an American stump-speaker, and yet he is not," I thought. "Where was he born?"

"I think I heard you say you were an American?" the Carlist continued.

"Yes."

"I'm not."

This was charmingly laconic. "I fancy that you are English."

The Carlist grew quite red in the face. I had evidently insulted him. "I am not English. I'm a Scotchman."

"I beg ten thousand pardons. I thought that since the merging of Scotland and England into the Kingdom of Great Britain this nice distinction had not been kept up, — at least on the Continent."

"Madam, you are entirely wrong. There is the greatest distinction between the two peoples. The English are very stupid and brutal. The Scotch are clever and are gentlemen. Wherever I go I say I am Scotch, and am received warmly."

"I congratulate you upon your good fortune.'

"My father is Scotch, and my mother is a Virginian. You are a Northerner, I suppose."

"Yes."

"I presumed as much. I fought all through the war on the Southern side. I was on General ——'s staff. The North treated us shamefully."

I laughed, and replied that, considering the South had been beaten, the North could afford to forgive hard words.

I thought the Scotch-Virginian Fire-Eater would have had a stroke of apoplexy.

"Beaten!" he roared. "Never! We were overcome, — overcome!"

"Be it so. I've no desire to dig up graves. The South fought well and was conquered; that is all. If you prefer Providence to the North, I'll say that Providence won the battle, and most deservedly."

The curl on that Fire-Eater's lip would have been a very Laocoön to me had it escaped, but fortunately it could not, and I still live. Silence ensued for the space of five minutes, and then, as if even a Yankee were better company than his own sweet self, the Fire-Eater lifted up his voice.

"Yes, I fought for the South, and I've been a Carlist for seven years. I'm here helping them, and any one who calls them boys does n't know what he is talking about."

"Pardon me, sir; I did not say that all Carlists were boys. I said that those I met were boys, and they were."

The Fire-Eater scowled. "Boys or no boys," he resumed, "we'll see whether the Carlists are beaten."

"I regret, sir," I said on rising, "that such good fighting material should be enlisted on the wrong side. Sooner or later Providence will be sure to defeat Don Carlos."

This was too much. The Fire-Eater swallowed some water, and in his rage choked. There was not a funeral the next day, so he did not die ; but was it not fitting that a believer in the divinity of Slavery should, in default of " niggers," devote his young vigorous life to the Divine Right of Bourbons ? Education has much to do with convictions, but I 'm beginning to believe that temperament has almost as much. Certainly temperament is largely responsible for what are called morals.

Where do you suppose the Blinker had gone to find my trunk ? At my banker's.

" How do you suppose good Mr. Banker could get it out of the custom-house without a key ?"

" But, madam, it was sent to his care ! "

O, that man was incorrigible. No amount of surgery could get an idea into his bullet head. " Come, we will go to the custom-house," I said ; and go we did, finding my poor little trunk sole occupant of a great room, looking as thin and unhappy as though its interior emptiness had broken out on the surface. The custom-house officer seemed to doubt the statement that there was nothing in the trunk, even after I offered to present him with its contents ; so opened it was, and when his eyes encountered nothing but a clothes-brush and a history of the Miracles at Lourdes, he gazed upon me with amazement.

"Madam, this is a mystery. American ladies travel with many fine clothes, — beaucoup, beaucoup, — and now I behold one who travels with a trunk and nothing in it. This world is strange !"

"The fact is," I answered, "my trunk had the cholera at Santander and lost flesh in consequence."

" Eh! qu'est-ce que c'est? Je ne comprend pas."

" C'est égal." And off I marched at the head of my army of trunk, borne on the shoulders of a porter who hummed the Conspirators' Chorus in " La Fille de Madame Angot," and remarked, as he deposited the light burden in my room, " It would be a good trunk to carry in hotter weather. What wealth of perspiration should I save!"

Now came the moment of eternal separation from the Blinker. It was a trying ordeal.

"Madam, it grieves me to part from you. For ten days you have been on my mind. I have felt for you in your trials. I have found you very amiable. I can say from my heart that you are very agreeable."

I bore up under this purely Blinkerian patronage, and smiled feebly.

"Yes, madam, I shall often think of you in that great country to which you will soon set sail, and it will be a great consolation if you give me your autograph, — only a few lines saying that you have been content with me, that in time of revolution I brought you safely into France, that I have lived twenty-six years in Spain — "

"Yes, yes, that will do." And I, like a coward, instead of telling that dirty, stupid, incompetent

12

man how utterly unfit he was for the position of courier, sat down and wrote thus : —

"The Blinker has been my courier for ten days. I suppose he is honest. He is said to be respectable. I know he is stupid, and if any one desires to cultivate the virtue of patience at considerable expense to his feelings and pocket, he cannot have a better opportunity than by securing the Blinker's services for a hurried tour through Spain."

The Blinker was delighted with my complaisance, and in backing himself out of the room, — for his manners improved the moment he had a favor to ask, — pronounced me "charming." I wonder what he thought when some obliging friend translated my recommendation.

When the door closed upon the Blinker's burly back I heaved a sigh of relief, sat down, and took a final survey of Spain. I had seen enough to know it were an impertinence to predict the future. Anything is possible. That there would be a change of government as soon as the Cortes met, was a matter of course. Spain has not improved

"The Blinker was delighted with my complaisance."

since Irving's day, when the Cabinet averaged two and a half revolutions annually.

"This consumption of ministers," writes the author of the Alhambra, "is appalling. . . . . To

carry on a negotiation with such transient func-
tionaries is like bargaining at the window of a
railroad car; before you can get a reply to a
proposition, the other party is out of sight." I
felt convinced that Castelar was too much of an
idealist to steer a wreck through stormy seas. He
had eaten, undoubtedly with the best intentions,
too many of his own words to command the confidence of extreme radicals or the respect of desperate enemies. Under the monarchy he had
many times demanded the suppression of standing armies and of the conscription. As Dictator
he upheld both. As independent orator he had
inveighed against the death-penalty. As Dictator he insisted upon its execution. In 1870
Señor Castelar was a Federal Republican, and
on the 11th of May of that year delivered a
famous speech wherein he said : —

"With the system of centralization, a single day, the
24th of February, 1848, decides the destiny of kings ; a

single night, the night of December 2, 1851, decides the destiny of states. In a country so constituted liberty is not a vivifying sunlight ; it is a flash of lightning, which strikes and vanishes. Government is not the pacific regulator of social life ; it acts like a blind and brutal force ; it oppresses, and it crushes. . . . . A short distance, from this hall to the Ministry of the Interior, and from that Ministry to the Palace of the Senate, covers the spinal marrow of a nation."

Three years later Castelar opposed federation, and made an enemy of the most sensible party in Spain, because it is the only one founded on *cosas de España*, the most pluperfectly Spanish *cosa* being provincial independence, and an inborn hatred of centralization. Now, Castelar thoroughly repudiates federal republicanism.

" Our convictions, our experiences, our sorrows, and our undeceivings, ay, even the very example of the most republican of countries, Switzerland and the United States, oblige us to condemn a banner and a policy under whose shadow the anarchical cantons were engendered, and to defend the only republic possible (*la republica posible*), — the one which is really traditional among us, — the one which considers the nationalities as total organisms whose private fragments cannot be decomposed or separated, even though but temporarily, without danger of death, — the one which places before everything and above everything the marvellous work of a thousand years, the unity and intgerity of our beloved Sapin."

That he should have abandoned federation is as mysterious as that he should have dreamed of regulating a brutal, ignorant people without an army or the death-penalty. To look at Spain for one moment from an ideal point of view is sheer madness in a traveller. What shall it be called in a statesman? Castelar is too pure a man not to be right in the end, and at no distant future he may learn the uselessness of poetry in politics, and the absolute necessity of founding convictions upon common sense. One thing seems certain. However distant peace may be to Spain, it never will dawn until the era of decentralization sets in. The Intransigenti know what they want far more definitely than do their opponents. They are in earnest, too, and Spain is likely to sink very much lower before she rises purified by fire and blood. Autonomy of the provinces they must and will have. As late as the reign of Isabella, Spanish coin described the Queen as sovereign of "the Spains." She was "Queen of the Spains." Aragon had one code, Castile another. Andalusia is totally unlike Galicia. The Basque provinces are given over to Carlism, — why? They became Carlists forty years ago because they were made to believe that if the constitution were established they would be put on a level with all the rest of Spain, whereas Absolute Monarchy would respect their privileges. They are Carlists to-day for the same reason.   Thirty-four years since Theophile Gautier wrote thus of Old and New Castile : —

" Balmaseda, Cabrera, Palillos, and other chiefs of more or less important bands, are subjects of perpetual discussion ; things are told of them that make one shudder, cruelties out of fashion, long since regarded as in bad taste among the Caribbeans and Cherokees. In his last move Balmaseda advanced within twenty leagues of Madrid, and having surprised a village near Aranda, amused himself by knocking out the teeth of the *ayuntamiento* and *alcade,* and finished the *divertissement* by nailing horseshoes to the hands and feet of a constitutional curé." (This last is now denied.) "As I showed my astonishment at the perfect tranquillity with which this news was received, I was told it happened in Old Castile, with which they did not concern themselves. This response covers Spanish ground completely, and furnishes the key to many things incomprehensible to us in France. In fact, an inhabitant of New Castile is as indifferent to what happens in Old Castile as though it were the moon. Spain does not exist from a unitary point of view ; there are always the Spains, Castile and Leon, Aragon and Navarre, Granada and Murcia, etc., — people who speak different dialects and detest one another."

Catalonia, the richest and most industrious of the provinces, has a history and language of its own. It is the Republicans of its chief town, Barcelona, who projected a federative Spain, it is Barcelona intelligence that feeds the Intransigenti with determination, and it is Barcelona that will probably dictate to the coming Spain.

Yes, the longer I sat thinking, the more I felt that Castelar would fall. Serrano and Monarchy would probably have their day to die at the hands of Intransigenti and Federal Spain. Serrano has since come to the surface ; but can such an adventurer benefit Spain? Can Castelar accept office under the man who aided Olozaga to defeat Espartero ; supported Espartero, and then abandoned him for O'Donnell ; assailed Narvaez, after working with him; welcomed Prim; drove away the Queen from whom he had received favors for which the meanest cur on four legs would have been grateful; became Regent in consequence; gave the crown to Amadeus; dethroned him when he was found to be an honest man; and finally escaped into France, disguised by wig and false beard? Invited to return to Spain by Castelar, whose faith in his countrymen does more credit to his heart than head, this political gymnast sends troops into the Cortes, dissolves the people's parliament, and proclaims himself Castelar's successor! Good came out of Nazareth, but good ought not to come out of Serrano, saving such as sometimes arises from making matters as bad as they can be. There is a certain sense of security in touching bottom, though that bottom be foul mud.

The rumble of discontent heard from one end of the Peninsula to the other is the most hopeful of all signs. Anything is better than stagnation, and this discontent among the low-down people denotes that, powerful as is the Church, its hold is less firm than ever before. There is an immense deal of infidelity among the peasants, and Castelar has told us that, though Spain destroyed herself to save Catholicism, giving for it all the blood in her veins and all the vitality of her spirit, there are but thirty-eight Spanish soldiers in the Pontifical army. This fact is enough to make Philip the Bigot turn in his coffin. Even the densest ignorance is not proof against the volcanic tendencies of this very uncomfortable century, which won't let any one enjoy a quiet life. Times have changed since Sancho Panza was snubbed by his wife for wanting to be governor of an island. "Dost thou live in peace, and let all the governments in the world go," said that practical dame. "Thou camest into the world without government, and thou mayest

be carried to thy long home without government
when it shall please the Lord.   How many people
in this world live without government, yet do well
enough, and are well looked upon !"

For that wretched woman, Isabella, whom every
one despises, I felt more pity than contempt.
First, what could be expected of a Bourbon?
Secondly, what human being, breathing the same
poisonous atmosphere from childhood, would be
any better?   Madame Ristori, who knew the
Queen well, and to whom she once appealed
successfully to save a soldier's life, assures me
that there was good in Isabella Second; and I
remember how charitably genial Irving looked
upon her exceptional position.

"You now see," he wrote privately, "in what a critical situation the poor little Queen is placed by being
declared of age. She has now to exercise the func-
tions of a sovereign while her mind is immature, her
character unfixed ; where she has no one at hand of

talent, integrity, and disinterested devotion to whom
she can look for counsel; where she is surrounded
by court flatterers and court intriguers of both sexes,
and where even her ministers are faithless."

Would any male Bourbon have been less blam-
able? And when Americans revile the second
Isabella, would it not be well to recall the first,
the sovereign to whose generosity we owe the
discovery of our continent? If a woman lost
Spain, a woman found America, and for her sake,
as well as for humanity's, I cry from my heart, —

"St. Jago and forward Spain!"

THE END.

www.ingramcontent.com/pod-product-compliance
Lightning Source LLC
Chambersburg PA
CBHW060613030726
47498CB00005B/1664